THE DEPTHS

THE DEPTHS

by
JOHN CREASEY

Walker and Company
New York

Library of Congress Catalog Card Number: 67-13245

First published in the United States of America in 1967 by Walker and Company, a division of Publications Development Corporation.

Printed in the United States of America from type set in Great Britain.

CONTENTS

PROLOGUE

1951. The medical conference on board the S.S. *Medici*, a fine new ocean-going liner, attracted enormous publicity. The governing bodies of the Chief Medical Organisation of the World had chartered the liner in order to make sure of secrecy during the discussions and the main sessions. The subject of the conference had leaked out a few hours before the liner set sail from Buenos Aires, for a week's cruise in the South Atlantic. The subject was of absorbing interest to all mankind, for it concerned the prolongation of the average life span. Several research groups were to announce their findings after twenty years of inquiry and experiment. Sensational stories circulated in all the world's newspapers. The S.S. *Medici* was in regular contact with the outside world, by radio, for the first five days of its cruise, and was last reported near Tristan da Cunha. Then all contact was broken. Air and sea searches were organised, the world was agog for news, but the S.S. *Medici* was never seen again. It was presumed sunk with all on board.

Some reports of a severe hurricane in the area persisted but no details were established.

1953. The S.S. *Olympic*, a new liner christened in the year of the Olympic Games in Japan, carried hundreds of the world's greatest athletes from great triumphs in the world of athletics. Russian, American, British, French, German, Japanese — gold medallists from many countries were on board on a torch-bearing cruise from Japan to Europe *via* New York. Radio contact was broken when the S.S. *Olympic* was three days out from New York. In spite of air and sea searches, the ship was not seen again. There was no news of any survivors.

A report from a French submarine of a violent storm in the vicinity was noted but there was no corroborative evidence.

1955. The S.S. *Venus of Milo*, an Italian liner of forty thousand tons displacement, was given the greatest send-off ever known for a liner, and received enormous space in the newspapers. On board were *Body Beautiful* teams from all of Europe, going to the United States for the World's Most Beautiful Body contest. Over six hundred of the world's loveliest girls and most handsome men were on board — each national group under the strictest supervision. The Press called the S.S. *Venus of Milo* the Beauty Boat. Newspapermen sent long, ecstatic reports home of the almost unbelievable convocation of perfect human bodies, until, four days out, silence fell. After the first surprise, alarm began to possess the organisers . . . and the alarm was fully justified, for no trace of ship, crew or the body beautiful passengers was ever found.

A radio ham, in Southern Ireland, reported picking up a message from the ship, very faintly. The message said: *"A tremendous wave is approaching the ship . . ."*

That was all.

1

THE PROFESSOR

No one seeing Professor Corvell for the first time, without knowing his name, would have had the slightest reason for thinking him remarkable — except for his nose. It was large and rubbery-looking, and on many men would have looked odd, even grotesque, but somehow it fitted in with the rest of his face. He had something of the appearance of a priest, a humble one, for his lips were full and soft and his cheeks were plump and pale and soft, his face was round and chubby, his hair a pale golden colour and very silky.

Anyone being abjured in a crowd to "look, there's Professor Corvell" would have been bewildered, and probably the last man selected would have been Corvell himself. He was so young. The aura of age and experience still hung about the word "professor" and if one did not think of Corvell as a priest, one thought of him as an overgrown schoolboy. He was in fact twenty-seven. He had been an infant prodigy in a restricted world yet one which had illimitable range — mathematics. At the age of sixteen he had nonplussed most of his tutors, at seventeen he had vanished, as it were, into the curious limbo of the nation's backroom boys. It was not only that he was a kind of human electronic computor; he had vision, which no electronic machine yet made had acquired.

Professor Corvell had first burst into prominence by accident. The Russians had sent another man into orbit, the Americans had followed suit, jubilation on both sides had been tempered by the fact that the other might have the first landing party ready for the moon. Then the professor had come out with his modest little statement:

"To ensure accuracy, of course, we need several space

stations between the earth and the moon, and I am glad to say that we are able, in this country, to put a space station into a stationary position and service it from earth *or* for the moon."

At first, no one believed him.

Then, suddenly, British Government policy permitted him to be interviewed on *Tonight*, later on *Panorama*, finally on *This Week*. Each appearance was spread further afield by Eurovision, and several television hams in North America picked up what he said, strongly. They even had the first trans-Atlantic picture of him. Moscow scoffed; Washington was cautious. With a daring which would have been inconceivable only a few months earlier, the government allowed Corvell to visit first Moscow to confer with Russian physicists, then Washington. The most renowned scientists on both sides admitted that Professor Corvell appeared to have solved one of the great problems of the space age.

On his return from the two trips, the professor came down on the side of American ice cream.

"It is not so much that it is better," he declared, *"but it has infinitely more variety."*

This was taken, correctly, as an indication that the government had decided that he had said enough; the other space age nations had, in a way, been warned. Professor Corvell dropped back into proper obscurity, one of the most famous and more enterprising ice cream manufacturers in the United States brought out its thirty-first flavour, *Professor C* — a luminous ice cream which glowed pink in the dark. Now and again references were made to the plump little man with the big nose and the sweet tooth, but he was no longer on the centre of the stage. What very few people knew was that Corvell had finished with space stations a long time before his statements; these utterances had been made (and approved by the government) to distract attention from his latest interest: the control of water. The uncontrolled and uncontrollable oceans of the world offered a new challenge. Always fascinated by hydro-dynamics, Corvell was toying with the fantastic calculations necessary to find out whether in fact the tides of the world *could* be made to stand still, or do what man wanted them to do.

For a long time before this interest Corvell was the central figure in the activities of Z5, the international secret organisation led by Dr Alexander Palfrey, with the Russian Stefan Andromovitch as his second in command. The reason for such prominence was simple. The Professor had become a kind of communal property. Each of the three major space age nations needed his knowledge and his potential, and those with vision believed that he was the greatest mathematician and physicist of his age — in fact of any age. Day and night, Z5 watched over him, not always with his knowledge. He was not a problem, as such. He realised a little of his own value to his own country, he had a proper international outlook, and he went nowhere without informing Palfrey's men. His pleasures were few. He was a teetotaller — not, he would say brightly, that he had any prejudice against alcohol as such, but he knew of nothing more likely to disturb mental judgement.

"*After all*," he would joke, "*it would startle you to see a large computer suddenly dancing a jig, wouldn't it?*"

He himself was quite light on his feet, and a much better dancer than most; he had a good sense of rhythm.

Then came the time of his nervous breakdown. . . .

*   *   *

The London and the British headquarters of Z5 had been moved, after the experience in *The Terror*, and were now underneath one of the great new commercial buildings in the heart of London. When the crowds had looked through the windows obligingly let into the wooden screens for the edification of the curious, no one had dreamed what was going to be put into the enormous hole. The ostensible purpose was of an impregnable vault, safer even than the Bank of England's, and only after it had been finished, the air-conditioning perfected, the lifts installed, the escape shafts built and the anti-radiation devices perfected, did Palfrey and his operatives take over.

Z5 had been under very great pressure for some time, since the defection of many of its English members. Palfrey had rebuilt the British — and incidentally the main European — headquarters in men, just as the governments of the major powers had rebuilt the structure with reinforced concrete. As far as it was humanly possible to be sure, every member — in fact everyone who stepped inside this place — was a perfect security risk; zero. There was a permanent staff of seventy, accommodation for eating and sleeping and for recreation for two hundred and fifty — against any time of emergency — and there was a floating population of agents from other parts of the world, often as many as twenty-five at any one time. It was a well-integrated little community. Some of its members spent weeks in the perfect air-conditioned atmosphere, without going up to the diesel-perfumed freshness of London. Others went up most days; there was no restriction on their movements except that imposed by their personal preferences and their work. Palfrey, who travelled a great deal, occasionally spent two or three successive days in the underground headquarters, and had come to regard such a sojourn as quite normal.

The secretariat of Z5 was comparatively small; there were fifteen persons in all. The Secretary-General was a tall, pale-faced, bright-eyed Scotsman, named Alec Merritt. Merritt had the same kind of mind as Corvell's, except that it was not tuned to the same mathematical perfection; the organisation mind. Next to his small office was a larger one which looked like the operations centre of a Service Ministry, and in fact it was an operations room. Instead of showing the position of hostile and/or unfriendly and allied naval air bases, aircraft, ships and missile bases and guided missiles, it showed the position of (a) Z5 agents throughout the world, (b) the position of men suspected of being potentially dangerous, and (c) men who had to be protected by Z5 because they might at any time be in some kind of danger.

Professor Corvell, of course, was one of these last.

He knew that Palfrey and Z5 were not secret service men in the normal sense; in a way they were in advance of the times.

During the second world war they had worked as an allied secret service, after the war they had been used to work against individuals and groups who were setting out to make excessive profits out of human misery, and also against any groups and individuals who had a Hitler mentality. In those early post-war days, it was surprising how many believed that some form of dictatorship was the best way of governing a country, and surprising how many individuals realised what enormous power one man (or a small group) could get into his own or its own hands with the right scientific advisers.

As the space age and the nuclear age developed, so the power which individuals could acquire increased. It was no longer necessary to try to blackmail the world, as Hitler did, with a nation armed to the teeth. It was possible to use a few comparatively small nuclear weapons based in remote parts of the world. It was Z5's task to seek out indications of any individuals or groups who sought such power, and to report regularly to those governments who helped to pay for the Department. It also had to watch men, like Professor Corvell, who were communal property.

A mind such as Corvell's could be very dangerous indeed if subjugated to hostile control. Palfrey's job was to seek out anyone who might attempt to harm, to injure or to corrupt him.

He well-remembered his first talk with the professor. He, Palfrey, was over a head taller, at six-feet one. He was a deceptively slender-looking man, with regular features, silky fair hair (that he had in common with Corvell) lazy-looking blue eyes with lids which seemed to droop a lot, as if he were sleepy.

"Just what do you do, Dr Palfrey?" Corvell had inquired, giving a cherubic smile. "Naturally I have heard a great deal about you, but — well, I return to my question. Just what *do* you do? I am told that I may safely place myself or rather my well-being, in your hands. I am *most* impressed."

Palfrey had looked at him thoughtfully.

"The national secret services look after the interests of their own countries, Professor — the Russians have theirs, the Americans theirs, every nation its own. The United Nations have a liaison with most of these, and a small organisation exclusive to it, which looks after the interests of the U.N., and advises where it is being threatened. Both are military and economic and — basically — political. Z_5 is not political. It is subsidised by the governments of a group of big and medium-sized powers to try to make sure that while they're looking after their own big fish, little fish don't start making trouble."

"And what would you regard as a little fish?"

"Any individual, group of individuals, corporations, political revolutionaries — virtually anyone who is *not* representing a government or a nation, and who might stir up trouble."

"I quite see the point," Corvell had said, rubbing his big nose and smiling happily. "I had no real idea. Supposing *I* were to be fired by some perverse notion, for instance——"

"Precisely."

They had both laughed.

Palfrey had met the little man several times since, and found him easy enough to get along with. All reports of him were satisfactory; his personal life — he was a bachelor — was quite beyond reproach. No one appeared to show any particular interest in him. He was one of the easier charges — until the time of that nervous breakdown. It showed in irascibility, in outbursts of temper, in failure to concentrate, and finally he collapsed when in his laboratory on the outskirts of London.

"Nothing organically wrong," the doctors declared. "He's been over-working, that's all. That kind of mind never knows when to stop. He must have a rest."

"Such as?" someone in authority had asked.

"Probably the best thing for him would be a long cruise," the doctors had answered.

This worried Palfrey, but he did not, at that stage, believe that he had sufficient grounds for advising the authorities not to agree. He had reported, of necessity, that none of his agents had been able to establish any cause other than accident for the loss of the *Olympic*, the *Medici*, and the *Venus of Milo*. Only

Palfrey, his friend Andromovitch and a few men high in the counsels of Z5 knew that Palfrey was worried in case there was a connection, beyond that of coincidence, between the sinkings. He would have liked to go on Corvell's cruise himself, but was too deeply involved in inquiries about other problems. However, he knew the Navy well enough to assume that exercises would be carried out near the ship — the S.S. *Seafarer* — for after all the Navy had to stage exercises somewhere. He sent one agent to be Corvell's steward on the S.S. *Seafarer*, placed another agent among the officers, and also sent Julia Shawn.

*   *   *

Julia Shawn, at twenty-six, was quite outstandingly attractive — that was why she had been selected — and absolutely reliable. She was briefed by Palfrey in his small, plainly furnished office deep beneath the throbbing heart of London.

"You have two jobs," Palfrey told her. "First, help Corvell to have as good a time as possible, remembering that this is a combination of convalescence and rest-cure. Second, watch anyone who appears to take too much interest in him."

"Do you think anyone will?" Julia asked.

"I think someone might," Palfrey answered, drily.

2

MEDITERRANEAN NIGHT

"What I can't understand, Julia," Paul Henson complained, "is what you see in that buffoon. He ought to be on the stage or in a circus."

"Perhaps he is, when he's not on a cruise," Julia said.

"Why on earth do you spend so much time with him?"

"He *is* a man," Julia answered.

The moment later, she wished she hadn't said that. Paul was

a little on the earnest side, but apart from that, she could hardly fault him. If she hadn't her job to do she would have spent much more time with him and much, much less with the professor, although she did not dislike Corvell. In fact, she had come to like him, almost from the moment he had leaned forward at the table which they shared with six others, touched her arm and beamed into her face.

"Do call me Timmy, won't you?"

Timmy . . .

He was an accomplished dancer, too; better than Paul, who hadn't a real sense of rhythm, only of discipline; he had been trained on the ballroom floor, Timmy was a natural.

"He's a clown," Paul retorted. "When you dance together it looks damned silly."

"It feels lovely," Julia said. "There aren't many men as light on their feet."

She was beginning to feel uneasy, because it looked as if Paul was going to try to force the issue, and she did not want him to become too serious — not yet, anyhow. She must allow nothing to distract her from her main job. At the moment she was off duty, as far as one could be on board this sleek, beautifully appointed ship sailing this smooth, beautifully moonlit sea. They were out of sight of the south of Europe and the north of Africa, in a world which was virtually their own. It was just after dinner. Timmy had gone down to his cabin; "*Just a little post-prandial relaxation, my dear, exactly what the doctor ordered!*" The Z5 steward was on duty, and would send word when Timmy left the main deck, where his cabin was amidships. The night air was soft, and translucent light put a sheen on Julia's dark hair, and seemed to give it a halo, put a sheen onto her dark blue eyes, and made her lips glisten.

"Julia," Paul said. She thought she detected stiffness of tone, as if this time he was really offended. "It's no use trying to needle me. I won't be needled."

That was better!

"It's the last thing I want to do. But Timmy's a much nicer little man than you think."

"Who is he?" inquired Henson.

"Timothy! A manufacturer of cheap-priced lingerie!"

"That's what he says he is," said Paul. "I've seen his face somewhere, and I can't place it. I've a feeling that he's very wealthy."

Julia laughed.

"Do you think I'm after his fortune?"

"As a matter of fact, I don't," Paul said. "But I think a lot of people do. I don't suppose it greatly matters to you what people think, but I hate to hear them talking about you. The latest rumour is——"

He broke off.

It did not matter, of course, and Julia didn't care; yet in a way she must, because she was annoyed. She felt the colour rise to her cheeks, and was glad that the light was so poor that Paul couldn't see that. She did not look away from him, and tried to keep her voice steady; the danger was that she might try too hard, and sound flippant. As she let these flashes of thought pass through her mind she realised that this man mattered to her more than she had thought. That was the only possible explanation of the fact that she felt so keenly about what he said.

"I'd love to hear the latest rumour," she said lightly.

"Forget it."

"Now, Paul. You can't whet my appetite and then snatch the tempting morsel away."

He did not speak for a moment, but at last put his hands forward, gripped hers, pulled her a little closer, and said in a hard voice:

"This is not funny. They say that you spend half the night in his cabin. If you do——"

"Paul, dear," Julia said very softly. "I think I ought to tell you what I think about you for even listening to such talk. And I know you ought to tell the gossips what you think of them, instead of coming and checking up on me." She pulled her hands free, but he tried to stop her. She was suddenly, furiously angry. "Let me go!"

He dropped her hands as if they were hot coals.

She turned her head, cheeks flaming, breath coming very quickly. She heard Paul cough, could imagine what he was feeling. Then two things happened to distract her — at that very moment when all her thoughts were on Paul, on rumour, on the reputation she had acquired on board the ship. She was just beginning to wonder why anyone should spread the scandal, whether it was simply a malicious-tongued bitch of a woman or a man she had disappointed, or whether it might possibly be an attempt to distract her from her main job. There was always the danger that a Z_5 agent might be known, and that deliberate attempts might be made to take her mind off her work; always the chance that someone knew who "Timmy Chitty" really was. There was even the possibility that Paul knew, and was deliberately upsetting her, so that she could not concentrate on her job. These thoughts were vague and confused, anger predominating — and at first she hardly realised that there was a vessel on the calm sea, not far away.

Then she noticed a silver shape, like a miniature submarine. It was several miles away, and moving fast, causing a sharp v of wake.

She could not see anyone on it. The silver craft puzzled her so much that momentarily she forgot Paul. Next moment, quite unexpectedly, the Professor appeared on deck, strolling along puffing at a cigar. He stood at the ship's rail, staring towards the little silvery boat.

"Julia," Paul was saying, "I'm terribly sorry."

She didn't answer.

"Julia——" he began again.

She glanced round. "Paul, what's that?"

"What's what?"

"Look, there. That boat?"

She pointed. The Professor was still leaning against the rail, and the end of his cigar glowed. The sea was so calm it was almost uncanny, and the moon shimmered on it as if on a mirror. There was the faint droning sound of the ship's engines; someone was walking about above their heads, on the games' deck; young couples, probably. No one else was up here on the boat deck, near the stern.

"It looks like a midget submarine," Paul said. "It's almost like a rocket missile, isn't it?"

Julia felt a stab of fear.

"It's gathering speed," said Paul. Excitement sounded in his voice — naturally he was glad of this interruption. He gripped her arm. "Look, there's a kind of window in that conning tower. It's damned odd. Surely one of the crew's seen it."

He looked about him. Julia saw the little craft gather speed, heading as if with uncontrollable speed towards the S.S. *Seafarer*.

Quite suddenly, there was a sharp cracking sound. Almost on the instant a great spout of water shot high into the air, like the blowing of a huge whale. It shot up in an enormous mushroom. The moonlight shimmered on it, but the iridescent light seemed to go dim. Water splashed against the side of the liner, then a tremendous wave followed.

"*Look out!*" cried Paul.

"*Professor!*" screamed Julia. "Pro——"

She began to run towards "Timmy", but Paul clutched her from behind, with an arm round her waist; it was like a steel band. She saw the Professor gaping at the wave as it came bearing down upon the ship, so huge that already its foaming crest towered above the level of this deck, and looked as if it would smash over the games deck, even over the bridge. There was a great hissing and roaring.

"*Professor!*" Julia screamed again. She scratched at Paul's hands, but he did not let go. She had a last glimpse of Corvell, hands raised, cigar dropping from his lips, gaping at the wave. Next moment, Paul got both arms round her, lifted her bodily, and flung her downwards towards one of the hatches. Somehow, he managed to break her fall. Before she realised what had happened, before she knew that she was face downwards on the deck, with him on top of her, the hissing reached screaming pitch and a great weight smashed down upon them both. She

felt Paul's hands drawn away from her body. She was
drenched, as if she had plunged fully dressed into the sea. The
frightening hissing sounds grew louder and louder. She was
flung heavily against the side of the gangway, banged her
head, and was sickened and dazed. The ocean tugged at her,
greedily. She felt herself floating in several feet of water and
knew that she was being drawn by the back-wash against the
rail and the sea. She felt panic, but had absolutely no control
over her movements. She could not see Paul or the Professor,
could see nothing except the pale green water of the sea, and
the strange lights upon it, caused by a silvery flash. Then she
banged up against the rails. Her legs slid underneath, but her
body jammed against the lower rung. The sea seemed to be
fighting for her, as if it wanted at all costs to drag her in, but
the rail held.

Sssssss-sssss, the water howled and screeched, as if it were
trying to terrify her. *Sssssss-sssss*. Then she realised that the
ship had heeled over on one side, it looked as if the sea was
coming up to meet her, to swamp her again; it looked as if it
was coming to engulf the great liner.

Then slowly, terrifyingly slowly, the ship righted itself. The
hissing sound kept on, but was less strident and less deafening.
Water spilled all about the deck, but it no longer pushed or
pulled Julia so tightly against the rails. She clutched the
bottom rail with her right hand. She was aware that she was
gasping for breath, that she had swallowed a lot of sea water,
that she was feeling sick — she *was* sick.

The ship rolled time and time again, but the degree of each
roll was less. Soon she was lying still on her side, on the soaked
deck. She could see the sea, which was almost calm again, and
lit by moonbeams.

Paul wasn't here.

Professor Corvell had vanished, too.

*   *   *

After a while, Julia heard voices. Slowly, painfully, she
hauled herself to her feet. She felt bruised and tender all over,

particularly on her right knee and at her forehead. She stood by the rail, clutching tightly; there was little movement of the ship now, she would be in no danger if she let go, and yet she dared not.

Men appeared; a ship's officer and a seaman. They came hurrying towards her. She recognised one of the junior engineers. He began to run, slipped on the wet deck, recovered, and reached her. He slid his arm round her waist, reminding her of Paul.

Paul.

The Professor.

"Are you all right?" The youngster gasped the words. "Are you — all right?"

"Yes, I——"

"Can you get below on your own?"

As he spoke, more men appeared, several of them in dinner-jackets, passengers who seemed to know what they were doing. A thickset, middle-aged man, came up and said:

"I'll look after her."

"How many — how many were swept overboard?" another man asked.

"Very few, sir. There wouldn't be many on deck at this hour. There's a man overboard alert, don't worry." The young engineer sounded positive. "And don't spread rumours, please."

The questioner's voice had a shrill edge.

"But there must have been——"

"If you can't keep quiet, get below," ordered the man who was helping Julia. "There can't have been many. He's quite right."

There had been Paul, tall, earnest, good-looking Paul. Oh, dear God! And there had been the Professor. Julia felt sick and dazed and frightened. She allowed the middle-aged man to take her as far as the first staircase landing; white-clad stewards were coming up, now, and two nurses appeared. A woman with a badly cut arm was saying:

"But I know she was up on deck, I'm absolutely sure." She

was about fifty, grey-haired, dressed in a glittering dress, wearing scintillating diamond rings, brooches, pins and earrings. She gripped Julia's hand, and blood from the cut spilled onto Julia's wet forearm and spread, a pale pink. "Were you up there?" A frightened face was thrust close to hers. "Did you see my daughter? She went up with a man."

There had been the footsteps, overhead.

"I haven't seen——" Julia began.

The woman pushed past her, a bald-headed man just behind her calling: "Maggie, she'll be all right. Don't get so worked up. She'll be all right." They disappeared.

A steward took Julia's arm.

"Like me to help you down, Miss?"

"No. I — I must see the Captain."

"You'll have to wait a little while, miss, he's pretty busy. Cor strewth, never seen anything like it in twenty years at sea. Never known a ship stand on her nose before."

Julia pulled herself free, and went along a narrow passage towards the captain's quarters. Stewards and junior officers barred her way, pale-faced, worried men. She was stopped near the radio office. The Radio Officer was a youngish man named Green; Julia had sent three radio reports to Palfrey already. Green was sitting at the huge control panel, with two assistants. A steward was saying:

"You can't go along to the captain's room yet, miss. If you'll go and rest——"

Julia pulled herself free, and thrust her way into the radio office.

"I must see Captain Smedley!"

The plump Radio Officer turned round, recognised her, stood up and said: "All right, Miss Shawn, I'll arrange it. But he won't have much time to spare. If I could give him a message," he went on, with hopeful cunning.

"I must find out if Mr Chitty is safe," Julia said. She knew in her heart that it was no use, Chitty must have been swept off his feet and into the sea; he must be drowned. But she could not tell Palfrey until she was absolutely sure.

The Radio Officer said: "I know that the Captain's ordered a search for him, Miss — everything possible will be done. I will get a call through to your London people as soon as I can. It shouldn't be long. Will you wait in your cabin?"

After a pause, she said: "I'll see if I can help down below."

She went down the stairs, holding onto the rail. Water dripped from her dress, which clung to her like a sheath; she did not give it a thought, and no one else paid much attention. On the stairs, on the landings, along the passages, injured people were lying. She helped two to sit up, two to their cabins. She went back to the promenade deck, where the *Crystal Bar* had been wrecked. Bottles had been flung all over the floor, chairs uprooted, glasses smashed, cocktail bits spread like snow all over the rich red carpet. A barman was sitting on one of the stools, and a nurse was dabbing at his forehead. Several women were helping the injured. A tall, lean officer came by as a passenger hurried along to him.

"Mr Chamberlain, please! My son was up on deck. Is he all right?"

"We're checking, sir," said the officer; the zig-zag gold braid told Julia that he was an engineer. "I think you'll find he's all right."

A woman was distraught because of her daughter, this man horrified because of fear for his son. People were hurrying to and fro. Music was being played — *dance* music. Julia passed the main lounge and saw people sitting back, some bleeding, some with their eyes closed. More stewards were rendering first aid, and she saw Bingo cards and Bingo pencils and Bingo call-balls all over the floor.

A snowy-haired old lady passed by, saying calmly to a frail old man:

"It could have been a real disaster, Joseph. Thank God it was no worse."

The Professor had been swept overboard.

"What do you think could have caused it?" the old lady

went on. "An earthquake, perhaps? Or an underwater explosion? Or——"

"We really mustn't guess, my dear," the old man said. "Let us go and see whether we can help."

3

THE SILVER STREAK

PALFREY was in his office.

He was planning to go up to street level, simply to walk through London on what he had been assured was a beautiful summer evening, with less traffic than usual about. It was ten o'clock. The day had been busy but not oppressively so; some cables from Moscow had arrived rather late, and he had stayed to help to decode them. They were not of major importance but it was never possible to be sure, and he liked to use every available moment.

He was more yawny than tired.

He was lonely, too. It was years since his wife, Drusilla, had died in that disaster which had killed so many, but from which the world had slowly recovered; the disaster by drought.* He had never since met a woman who stirred his interest, still less desire, and on these lonely nights he would remember the deep contentment of life with Drusilla, and would wonder what his future held. His son, thank God, had lived. He was on the other side of the world now, doing some research work on Australian aborigines — as if he wanted to help make sure that whatever posterity came into being, they would at least have a full history of mankind in Australasia.

Yes, Palfrey was lonely.

He opened his door, walked along a narrow passage, and opened the Secretary-General's. Merritt was not there. A youngish woman, who had become Merritt's right-hand man

* *The Drought* — an earlier story of Dr Palfrey.

as it were, and might one day become even more to him, was sitting at the big plain desk. She was Joyce Morgan. On the wall by her side was an instrument panel, which was connected with the operations room next door.

She looked up, and smiled brightly.

"Hallo, Sap. Going up for air?"

"Think you could spare me for an hour?"

"Of course," she said. "I wish you would go upstairs more than you do."

"And you wish Alec would, too!"

She laughed. She was attractive, nicely made-up and well dressed in a summerweight suit of pale red. She had come into Z5's service at the time of *The Terror*, when her father and her brother had been among those who, having been corrupted, had ranged themselves against the national interests. In the past year she had become absorbed in her work; anyone who stayed long in Z5's service did. It had to become a form of dedication, or one was useless.

"Yes, I wish Alec would go and look at the sun sometimes," she admitted. "Sap, will you try to make him take a holiday this summer?"

"I'll do more. I'll make him."

"Don't let him realise that it is a holiday," she warned, as an afterthought. "He'll enjoy it much more if he thinks he's working."

How well she knew Alec Merritt!

Palfrey went out, and walked along a narrow passage to one of the exit shafts. There were no staircases here, only lifts and shafts. The lifts were large enough only for three people at a time; they were really tiny automatic lifts, fitted with hand-operated pulleys so that if there was at any time any serious breakdown in electricity or any failure with the electronics system under which headquarters operated, individuals could go up to safety in the street, or to higher levels in the underground building. Palfrey had reached Shaft 17 when a white light shone above it — and a white light meant a call for him. He moved to the telephone which was built into an alcove at waist level; telephones were placed all about the intricate system of passages and offices so that no one need be out of touch for more than a few seconds.

"Palfrey."

"Sap, come back, will you?" It was Joyce. "I've just had a flash that something has happened on board the *Seafarer*."

"I'm on my way," Palfrey said quickly.

He had been used to this kind of situation for years; it seemed sometimes as if he had never known the day when emergency did not threaten. He ought to be inured to it. Instead, his heart began to thump as he strode back towards the Secretary-General's office and the control room. He had a mind picture of the man who mattered on the ship: Professor Corvell. Then he reminded himself of the Z5 agents who were also on board. "Something has happened" could mean anything, and he did not try to imagine what.

He turned into the office. The door was open, and a junior official was standing-in for Joyce, who must be in the control room. Palfrey stepped inside. Half a dozen operatives were on duty, each wearing ear-phones. Messages from all over the world arrived here, minute by minute — in a way it was like the Information Room at New Scotland Yard, except that there was seldom the same sense of urgency. Now, there was. Joyce had ear-phones at her head, but as Palfrey entered she took them away, and said:

"Broadcast, please."

Immediately, a voice sounded from one of the loud speakers set round the walls. The voice sounded tinny and remote, but the words were crystal clear. It was a man.

"Our position is Latitude 42° 55′ N. Longitude 06° 25′ E. We are not damaged below the waterline and apart from incidental damage and injuries to crew and passengers there appears to be no damage above the waterline. The cause of the incident is not known. Hold on, please." There was a pause.

Joyce said clearly: "They were hit by a giant wave, something like a tidal wave. Several passengers and some members of the crew were swept overboard, and there is little hope of saving them."

Palfrey asked stiffly: "The Professor?"

"I don't know, yet."

Palfrey nodded, and his gaze strayed to one of the panels set in the wall on his right. This was a map record of disappearances. Most of the men and women named on the board were agents of Z5, a few were people who were to have been protected, some were scientists, chemists, physicists and mathematicians, experts in many fields. All had vanished. At one time, such a vanishing trick would have carried the assumption that the man — or woman — had deliberately crossed beneath the iron curtain, or else had left Russia for the West. This was no longer so. Men like Professor Corvell worked under conditions of great strain. Their minds were already tuned to such a pitch of nervous tension that collapses were commonplace, loss of memory was almost as frequent, and short-term disappearances not unremarkable. Yet some of the disappearances in recent months had become more than short-term; some men and women as important in their sphere as Corvell had been missing for a long time.

Palfrey had been checking on some, and had asked Merritt for more reports.

One common factor was revealing itself in these reports; a surprisingly high proportion of those who disappeared had last been seen at or near a coastal resort; some had last been seen swimming, or in a small boat. None of them had been traced.

He put this out of his mind and began to wonder why there had been no report from the Admiralty.

The voice came over the air again.

"*This is the master of the S.S. Seafarer calling London. I am now in a position to give a preliminary list of casualties and of disappearances. Twenty-seven passengers are suffering from broken limbs, two of them are seriously injured. One hundred and ninety-eight are suffering from cuts and bruises. Some members of the crew are missing. Eleven members of the crew have suffered broken limbs, the total slightly injured has not yet been computed. There is no damage in the engine room, and conditions now appear to be normal. The sea is calm. One moment please . . . I am now able to give you the names of seven passengers known to be missing. Each was on deck at the time we were struck by the wave, and none has been seen since.*

"*Mr Timothy Chitty . . .*"

Palfrey's hands clenched. Joyce Morgan moved to his side, as if she understood what he was feeling. He forced himself to listen, for there were three Z5 agents on board that ship, each looking after Chitty; one or more should have been near him.

The master was continuing: "*Miss Muriel del Spiro, Mr Juan Fernando, who were known to be together on the sports deck. Mr Paul Henson, Mr Henry Gibson, Mrs Jennifer Townsend, Mr Maurice Owen. Reference to the passenger list is recommended for further details.*

"*I am making for Nice, to disembark the seriously injured passengers, and will report again each hour on the hour.*"

The loud speaker fell silent. The control room operatives, some of them listening on their ear-phones to messages from other parts of the world, all watched Palfrey; everyone here knew that Corvell was the most important charge the organisation had; it would be impossible to receive worse security news than this.

Palfrey thought exactly the same.

There was a chance, of course, that Corvell would be picked up, but it was very slim. He took a sheet of paper from Joyce. It showed the time of the great wave, the time of the first report from the ship, and times of other messages; so far no bodies had been discovered. The Admiralty as well as the Naval Squadron on manoeuvres in the Mediterranean must have had this message by now. Why——

Joyce looked up.

"Admiral Correson is on the line, Sap."

Palfrey took the telephone.

"Thanks. Hullo, Corry. What news have you got for me?"

"None you're going to like," the Admiral told him. "That wave was the result of an underwater explosion. There is some evidence of radiation-clean particles in water and the air. We had ships within fifteen miles, but had no warning. Our radar reported some small craft near the *Seafarer*, and one of them showed more clearly than most — as if it had a very bright surface. Certainly no large surface vessels and almost certainly no submarines were in the vicinity."

"What chance of survivors?" asked Palfrey.

"Poor — especially at night."

"All right, Corry, thanks," Palfrey said bleakly. "You'll put in your reports that I asked you to keep your eyes open, won't you?"

"Sap — what do you *know* about this?"

"Nothing," answered Palfrey. "I don't even know what I fear."

He rang off, nodded to Joyce, and went into his own room. He did not let himself admit it to anyone else, but he was frightened.

He opened a drawer in his desk, and pulled out a chart, rolled up to save space. He spread this out on the desk, and weighted the corners with a paperweight, a pen, a book and an inkstand. Then he studied it closely. It was *Geographia's Oceans of the World*, and was completely incomprehensible to a layman, but he had studied it too often and too long to be puzzled by it now. All about it were little red dots, and among the places indicated with such dots were Tristan da Cunha, the coast line of Texas where a hurricane had struck with fiendish force not long ago, the north coast of Japan, the coast of British Honduras. There were many more red dots, and each represented what might loosely be called a "tidal wave". In most cases the cause was known, or believed to be known. Was it?

Some were known beyond doubt, of course; three hurricanes had been traced far out in the Atlantic and the Pacific Oceans and followed all along their course. Two earthquakes had taken place on the known fault areas, and there was no reasonable doubt about them. But there were others which it was impossible to be sure about; small waves which might be due to some form of natural phenomena, and which could be man-made. Palfrey brooded. Years ago, he had worked against a group of power-seeking men experimenting with underground atomic explosions, and creating "earthquakes"; at that time, before the full might of nuclear explosions had been known, a hundred-megaton bomb had not been thought of. Underground tests had become so commonplace these days that none but the angry or the frightened gave them much thought.

Z5 agents had checked, with experts, in every case. Seven of the waves had no known natural cause, and each of these had been what Admiral Correson called local.

Someone could control the seas, at least to some degree.

Palfrey had completely forgotten his decision to go "up" to London's surface. There was too much to do. Whitehall, Washington and the Kremlin had to be informed, and he put in radio telephone calls to his agent in each distant city. Each took the news calmly, each promised to pass it on. He called 10 Downing Street on a private line; the Prime Minister was out, but his first secretary said:

"This is going to upset him badly, Palfrey. Corvell is one of our most important cards."

"Don't I know it," Palfrey said.

"Is there no chance at all that he's alive?"

"I suppose there's a chance," Palfrey conceded. "It's a slim one, but it exists. I'll keep you posted."

"I certainly hope you will," the first secretary said. "Thank you for calling so promptly."

Palfrey rang off, reflecting almost sourly that everything essential had been done — except the hard thinking. He pulled the chart and reports towards him and began to study them. He was still deeply troubled. When he had absorbed all there was to learn from the details he crossed to another filing cabinet, and took out reports of a different nature; of men who had vanished off the face of the earth or the oceans.

Like the Professor——

Then Palfrey began to wonder why Julia Shawn had not

reported. He was beginning to worry when a light flashed on his desk. He lifted the telephone, and was told:

"A call for you from SKJ, sir."

This was Julia.

4

PHENOMENA

"Yes, I was actually on deck," Julia Shawn said. "I saw him just before he was swept off the ship. I don't think there is really any chance at all that he will be picked up. I don't see how he can be."

She was in a small cabin next to the radio office, with ear-phones clipped over her head. Apart from a faint droning sound, all she could hear was Palfrey's voice; there was no interference from atmospherics. The ship was moving with almost unbelievable smoothness which made the awful wave seem like something which had happened in a nightmare. She was feeling much more in command of herself, over the worst of the emotional effect of what had happened. Above every-thing else when talking with Palfrey, she had to be objective and detached; there was no room for the luxury of emotion, one had to force that aside when working for Z5.

Palfrey's pleasant voice had an engagingly casual tone; nothing could be more calculated to ease tension.

"So you saw everything happen, you really were on the ball. Can you describe it to me?"

"Yes, vividly," she said, and did so. When she talked of the silver streak which had looked rather like a tiny rocket missile or a midget submarine, the picture came back. She could almost hear the hiss and roar of the water.

When she had finished, Palfrey said: "I'll come out and see you." Something in his voice told her that he thought what she had said was of utmost importance. "I want you to take extreme precautions, personally. Are the other two all right?"

"Simon is badly bruised. Morris seems perfectly all right."

"Tell them what I say," said Palfrey. "You are to take extreme precautions. Stay on board until I arrive. I'll make sure that the ship stays in Nice long enough——"

"From what I hear it will be staying for several days. There's hardly a piece of unbroken crockery left on board," Julia said. "All right, I'll be careful."

"Julia," Palfrey said softly, "take *very* great care."

After a pause, she answered: "Yes, I will. Is that all?"

"I'll see you in about four hours' time," Palfrey said, and hung up.

She took the ear-phones off, slowly. Palfrey's quiet, calming voice had changed so much that he had alarmed her; he had meant to, of course. In some way he had read acute danger for her into what had happened. Her mind, trained to follow such reasoning, trained not to overlook any indications which might help to answer a problem, was blank for a few seconds. She did not go out of the cabin, where there was a small desk, two chairs, and some filing cabinets. What made him think that she was in danger? What had she said——

She began to smile, her lips stiff and taut. It wasn't very difficult to find the answer. She had seen that silvery streak, seen the whole incident — and as far as she knew, no one else who had been on deck was alive. It was like Palfrey to see the possible significance of that so quickly.

She lifted a ship's telephone, and called for Simon — the engineering officer on Z5's staff. It was several minutes before he came to the telephone. She told him precisely what Palfrey had said, and she could not rid her mind of the fear which Palfrey had put into it.

Simon was brisk, young, assured.

"The best thing is to lock yourself in your cabin," he said. "I'll come up for you. Don't see why there should be any danger on board, but if the great man says do a thing, we do it. I'll be up in a few minutes. Stay put, won't you?"

She sat in the little bare room, able to hear the droning beat of the engine. Now and again, she also heard squawks and squeaks from the radio room next door. There had been a regular stream of passengers who had sent off radio telegrams, and everyone on board had been excessively busy for the past two hours. A great deal of tidying up had already been done, but the main lounge was rather like the waiting room of a hospital after a big train crash. She did not know how many people had been seriously hurt, but there were a great many. She opened her bag and lit a cigarette. Simon was a long time, but any number of things might have delayed him. She found herself brooding over Z5 and its organisation. There was hardly a ship afloat, there was no airfield of consequence, no city of any size, no railway station, no big factory, in which there was not a Z5 agent. Comparatively few were full time; most, like Simon, did their normal daily job, and worked as observers (and in emergency as active operatives) in their off duty hours. Simon could switch from spare to full time at any moment, she knew; the Captain almost certainly believed that he was in the British Secret Service; the Captain doubtless thought *she* was, too.

Where *was* Simon?

She finished the cigarette. It had been nearly a quarter of an hour since he had said that he would be along in five minutes, and whatever the cause of the delay, this was surprising. Should she try to get him on the telephone again? If he had been delayed, surely he would have called her. She watched the hand of her wrist watch moving barely perceptibly, for a full sixty seconds. She stepped towards the door, but hesitated. Take extreme precautions, Palfrey had said — and Simon had made it clear that he meant her to obey. She picked up the receiver again; the ship's operator was a long time answering. When at last the girl did, she said:

"I'll try to get him for you."

Julia put the receiver down again. Her heart was thumping with that fear which Palfrey had inspired and which this long delay heightened so much. It wasn't like Simon, big, boyish, bustling Simon, the popular type of public schoolboy. He was always so prompt.

There was a tap at the door.

She swung round towards it, expecting to hear Simon call out, but he did not. She hesitated, then moved across the cabin. The knock came again; heavy, peremptory; but if it were Simon, why didn't he call out? She touched the handle of the door.

The knock came for the third time.

"Who is it?" she called.

A man called back: "It is I — Simon!"

She knew, on that instant, that it wasn't; Simon would have said: "*It's me, open up!*" She turned slowly towards the telephone again, lifted it gingerly so that it did not make much noise, and prayed that this time the operator would not be so long. It was useless to ask for Morris, the Z5 steward, but she had to call someone on whom she could rely. The operator answered as the man outside thumped on the door again.

"Give me the Radio Officer, quickly," Julia whispered.

"I'm sorry, I can't hear you."

"*Radio Officer, quickly.*"

"Very good, miss."

He might be engaged.

"One moment, please." There was only a moment's pause, before a man answered — and as he did so the man outside called in that un-Simon-like voice:

"Julia, please. Open the door — at once."

"Want me?" asked the Radio Officer.

"Please," Julia said, with soft urgency, "send someone to see who is outside my door. He claims to be Simon Alting, the Third Engineer, but I don't think he is."

"I'll come myself — I'm just going off duty," the Radio Officer said briskly.

Julia heard his telephone go down. She listened intently for another bang at the door, but it didn't come. She thought she heard a squeaking sound, but that stopped. Suddenly, a voice was raised:

"Just a moment!" That was the Radio Officer. There were thudding footsteps, followed suddenly by a rumble of sound, a couple of hearty expletives, and noises which were more subdued. After a moment, there was another bang on the door, and the Radio Officer called: "I missed him. What's the trouble, Miss Shawn?"

She opened the door.

"Simon Alting was coming up to see me," she said. There was no need to go into details, the Radio Officer and all of the ship's officers knew that she had to have special treatment. "I can't understand what kept him. And this man——"

She broke off.

"Funny business," remarked the Radio Officer. Although he had been swamped by the work that evening, he looked as bright and fresh as if it were early morning, and he was facing the new day. "Anything I can do?"

"I'd like to go down to my cabin."

"Can I walk you down?"

"Please."

"It will be a pleasure," he said. "I've just got to pop my nose in next door." He slid his arm through hers, comfortingly, and they went outside, the Radio Officer talking all the time. "The chap must have realised that you'd rumbled him. He was disappearing round the corner when I reached the door. I just saw his heels. I fell over a dumb-bell from the gymnasium — nothing in this ship is where it should be, tonight." Still holding her arm, he looked into his office. "I'll be back in an hour, Jim." The man named Jim called back, and the Radio Officer marched Julia along the passage to the nearest lift; it opened as they reached it, and the Captain and two passengers stepped out. Julia recognised the passenger who had been trying to reassure his anxious wife.

"You can be sure that every — *everything* is being done, sir."

"But we should have turned back. I tell you it was criminal not to!"

"Two British destroyers and one French know our exact position, and fishing boats from Algiers are also searching," the Captain said in a flat voice. He nodded to Julia as they passed. Julia stepped into the elevator, where a one-armed liftman waited, a patch of plaster over his right eye.

"Never known anything like it since I was blown up in the second world war," he remarked. "On the oldest ship in the navy, that was. I was riddled with shrapnel and shell splinters. But you did know what you was in for——"

"You haven't seen Mr Alting about, have you?"

"Third Engineer? Haven't you heard?"

Julia's heart began to beat fast again.

"What should I have heard?" asked the Radio Officer.

"Fell down one of the ladders in the engine room, and split his head right open. Had twenty stitches put in, they tell me. Never rains but it pours."

"*Fell*," echoed the Radio Officer.

"Think he's been at sea long enough to know how to climb up and down a steel ladder, wouldn't you?"

The lift stopped at A deck, two below Promenade. Julia stepped out. The Radio Officer's fingers were tight on her arm — almost painful. As the elevator doors slid to behind them, and they were alone for a moment, he said:

"What's going on, Miss Shawn?"

"I wish I knew."

"Someone after you?"

"It looks like it."

"We'll go along to your cabin, and I'll put one of the sergeants-at-arms on duty, until you're quite safe," the Radio Officer promised. "Don't worry." But he himself looked worried. They went briskly along to her cabin, A49, which had a porthole. He took the key from her, unlocked the door, and said: "Wait there a moment." He went inside. Someone came hurrying along the passage, a youngish man whom she had noticed several times, and fear clutched her again, but he passed with a brisk:

"What a night!"

"Yes, isn't it?"

The Radio Officer reappeared.

"I've looked in the bathroom, behind the shower, under the bed and in the wardrobe — the cabin's quite empty. Lock yourself in. I'll bring the man to look after you myself — don't worry any more."

"You're very good."

"Got to look after our VIP's," he said, and grinned; in spite of the quickness with which he acted and his seriousness he was lively and light-hearted. "You look as if you're nearly all in," he said. "You ought to lie down."

"I think I will."

"Wise girl." He stepped outside, pulling the door to as he went, and she saw his pale plump hand on the handle, the braid of his sleeve. Then she heard him cry out in sharp alarm: "*Lock the door!*" This was the kind of situation for which she had been trained absolutely. All human impulse would be to try to help the man outside, but she had to save herself because of what she could tell Palfrey, and Z5.

There was a clatter of running footsteps followed by a sharp snap of sound which she didn't recognise but which filled her with terror. She flung herself at the door. It slammed. She caught sight of a man outside, a tall man backing away from the Radio Officer, who had flung himself forward. She saw blood crimson on the Radio Officer's right cheek, before the door slammed and cut them off from sight. She thrust her finger on the safety lock, and heard it click home. There was a shriek outside, another sharp snap, a shout, and more thudding footsteps. Muted voices sounded. She stood close by the door, body tense, hardly breathing.

A man said: "My God, he's dead."

5

MEETING

PALFREY leaned forward in his seat, close to one of the little round windows of the aircraft, and looked down onto the city of Nice and the darkness of the sea beyond. The moon had set. Few street lights were on. Only here and there lights glowed from houses, but there was sufficient light in the sky for him to see the outline of the great hotels on the Promenade des Anglais, showing up ghostly white; some of the villas on the corniches showed up in the same eerie way. A few cars moved along the main roads, headlights showing. The only welcoming oasis of light in this early morning darkness was at the harbour, and there he could see the S.S. *Seafarer*, a blaze of white and coloured lights. Arc lamps were ablaze on the dockside, too. As the plane lost height, Palfrey could see the covered gangways between the ship and the quayside, and actually saw two stretchers being carried, and could make out the whiteness of the ambulances waiting to take the injured to hospital.

He had received the latest list of casualties while in the air. Three more passengers and one additional member of the crew were seriously injured. No one else was reported missing. He knew that he would be met with an up-to-the-minute report as soon as he reached the airfield — young Simon would bring it in person. As the aircraft lost height the blaze of light faded from his line of vision, and was no more than a glow. Now the runway lights almost blinded him. He sat back with his eyes closed. Patience was forced upon him, but was not easy. He was so desperately anxious to hear everything Julia could tell him.

He had sent out a coded message to all the world's key agents and to all agents at sea ports, coastal cities, and on sea-going ships, asking for any reports of phenomena such as Julia had described. He might have to amend the description when he had talked to her, but it would be substantially the same. He had made a special point of asking agents near the spots where there had been tidal waves without any apparent natural explanation — reports might begin to come in while he was at Nice. Z5's agent in Nice ran a small fleet of pleasure and fishing craft, which he hired to Riviera visitors; he was a small, portly man named Duval, Henri Duval, who would almost certainly be waiting for word from Palfrey but would not be at the airport; probably no one outside the secretariat in London knew that he served Z5. He had also sent a message to Simon Alting, whose main job on board the

Seafarer had been to look after Julia. Simon should be at the airport.

They touched earth, bumped, ran more smoothly, and gradually slowed down. Spotlights shone on ambulances and fire tenders, standing over by the main airport buildings, where other lights glowed. A few people were standing about. The plane, a Dakota which ferried luxury foodstuffs to and from England and the Riviera, was a regular flight; there was nothing abnormal in a passenger being on board — it happened that he was the only one, tonight.

The co-pilot came up to him.

"Not a bad flip, sir."

"Very good," agreed Palfrey. "Not my idea of a regular night's entertainment, but I couldn't have asked for it smoother."

"Got to earn the old living somehow," the co-pilot said. "Good-bye, sir."

They shook hands.

Palfrey stepped down the ladder from the cabin, looking at the little group of people standing there. They were waiting to unload the cargo of course, and the belly doors were already gaping open. He did not see Simon, and no one approached him. That was puzzling. He followed a man who said: "*Douane, m'sieu, par ici.*" It was pleasantly warm, and there was a delicate scent on the air, as if bougainvillea and geraniums were growing close by. A gentle breeze came off the sea. He went into the Customs shed, where a man in a blue boiler suit stood in solitary state behind a huge, empty bench.

"You have something to declare?"

"Nothing at all," Palfrey said. He showed his card, and the man said:

"*Votre pardon, m'sieu.*" He chalked white crosses on Palfrey's one suitcase. Palfrey went out. Why wasn't Simon here? Why was no one here from the ship? He had not made special arrangements except to tell Simon to look after the girl, and to come and meet him. The disquiet which Palfrey had felt from the beginning of the affair increased.

No taxis were waiting, but a car came sweeping up, its headlamps swaying. It stopped alongside Palfrey, and he thought: The fool's left it late. Then the door opened and a tall, very thin man jumped out — not Simon Alting, but Morris, the steward who had been looking after Professor Corvell.

"Very sorry I'm late, skipper." Morris had a Cockney accent and somehow the face of a Cockney, with bony features, rather deep set eyes. "Had a bitta trouble at the last minute. Going to sit in the back or by my side?"

"I'll sit next to you," said Palfrey, and got in. Morris slammed the door as if it were made of steel, and the whole body of the car, a Citroen, shuddered. He snatched the wheel. "Good trip, sir?"

"Yes. What's happened?"

"Simon fell off a ladder in——"

"*Fell?*"

"Or was he pushed?" Morris switched on the engine, and thrust his foot on the accelerator. "No one knows. He was near the top. Could've slipped, or some swab could've trod on his fingers. Never can tell who's among the crew, can you? His fingers are a bit bruised, but cuts and bruises are ten a penny on the good ship *Seafarer* tonight. Cut his head open something awful. Concussed, too, but the docs say he'll be all right. I just come from the hospital, that's why I'm a bit late."

Palfrey felt almost icy cold.

"Miss Shawn?"

"She's okay, but someone had a coupla attempts to kill her. Got the Radio Officer instead. I tell you, this has bin some night. . . ."

*   *   *

Julia Shawn seemed composed enough when Palfrey entered her cabin, half an hour later. She was freshly made-up, her hair had been combed back, and her fine, clear cut features were shown to advantage. She had clear, rather dark blue eyes, finely marked brows, a chin that was a little too pointed. The most noticeable thing about her was her flawless complexion, slightly olive, beautifully coloured. Knowing what she had been through in the past few hours, Palfrey told himself that she had recovered extremely well. Emergencies and crises always brought out the worst or the best in an agent; he did not think he would ever have to worry what kind of job Julia was assigned to.

Fruit juice, hot buttered toast and hot coffee were brought in almost in Palfrey's wake.

"Tell me everything as we have breakfast," Palfrey said. He leaned back in one of the small easy chairs, watching Julia, and his right hand strayed to his forehead. He twisted a few strands of hair round his forefinger, and kept twirling it slowly, as she talked. It was five minutes before she stopped.

Palfrey did not move, even his hand went still.

"This silver streak — exactly what was it like?"

"Well — I first thought it was a motor boat. One of these modern, very streamlined ones, made of aluminium. It shimmered in the moonlight. Afterwards, I thought it might be a rocket. A passenger who was with me thought it looked like a midget submarine."

"Did anyone else see it?"

She hesitated, but Palfrey did not try to hurry her.

"Yes," she said at last. "Corvell did. And the passenger, Paul Henson, did." She had told him in reports about Henson, and did not need to explain who he was. "I'm sure about that. The Professor almost certainly did, too, but I can't swear to it. I don't know about the couple who were on the deck above, but I think they were on the other side of the ship."

Palfrey said: "And the noise? Did it come from the silvery streak?"

Again, she hesitated, while Palfrey told himself that she was making quite certain that she told him the precise truth — she was not going to allow herself a single unconsidered statement. Very slowly and deliberately, she answered:

"I don't think so."

"Why do you say that?"

"The silver thing was moving very fast," she explained. "It

was heading for the ship's side — just for a moment I thought it might be a kind of torpedo. Then the noise came. After that came the wave."

"After the noise?"

"Oh, yes. Seconds afterwards."

"Did you see the silvery streak after the wave?"

"No."

"Are you quite sure?"

"I am positive."

"When was the last time you saw it?"

"It was heading for the ship — I suppose it was fifty or sixty feet away. It gathered speed suddenly. There was a great mushroom of water, and the next thing I saw was the wave, towering over——" she broke off. "I *think* I remember thinking that if the silvery thing was a boat, then it would be smashed to pieces against the side of the ship, but I don't remember seeing it, or hearing any other sound except the hissing of the water. When the wave hit us, I was trying to move towards the Professor, but Paul Henson flung himself at me and held me down. If he hadn't, I would have been carried away. Like he was."

"Did you see anyone in this boat-like object?"

"No. Paul said he thought there was a window in the kind of conning tower, but he didn't say he noticed anyone. I certainly didn't."

"How big was it?"

"As big as a small motor boat."

"Are you sure that Professor Corvell saw it?"

"I assume that he did. I know that he saw the wave — he was standing gaping at it, his hands up in the air" — she demonstrated, with the palms of her hands thrust close to Palfrey's face — "as if he were trying to fend it off. He looked thunderstruck."

"I can imagine it," Palfrey said. "Now, about these attacks on you——"

She described them with the lucidity and precision with which she had told him the rest of the story. Only now and again did her fear show through; most of the time she was completely composed, and her voice seldom trembled. It did when she explained how a man outside had cried: "*My God. He's dead.*"

"And after that three men were stationed outside the cabin all the time — they were when you came in, weren't they?"

"Yes."

"Sap——" she began, and broke off.

He watched her steadily, intently. She pressed her hands against her forehead, then lowered them slowly.

"Sap, do you think they tried to kill me to prevent me from describing what I saw?"

"Can you think of another reason?"

"No."

"But it means that they had——" she broke off again, obviously much more agitated than she showed. "I keep thinking 'they'. Who *are* they? Who would want to do a thing like this? Who would want to drown Timmy? Who would be so ruthless? And if that isn't enough — *how* did they do it?" When Palfrey made no comment, she went on: "Of course, we know the answer to that, don't we? They exploded a radiation-clean nuclear bomb beneath the water. I — I've heard that three small ships were wrecked, probably thirty people have died. Why should they be so ruthless? Why should they care so little about the effects of what they're doing?"

Palfrey spread his hands.

"Look at it another way," he said. "Until tonight, we didn't know anyone was being ruthless, we didn't know that anything sinister was happening — we simply didn't suspect the existence of any 'they'. This is the first real step forward we've been able to make — now we know they exist we can start looking for them. You were in at the start, but they will know you've reported everything to me, so you should be out of danger."

"*Out* of danger?"

"Yes, of course," Palfrey reasoned. "They can no longer hope to stop you from reporting everything. Unless they are prepared to kill out of sheer spite, you'll be all right on that score." He patted the twist of hair onto his forehead; it made a wispy kind of kiss-curl. "Now! Whoever attacked you, killed the Radio Officer and pushed Simon down the ladder, has almost certainly escaped. It might have been a passenger, but could have been one of the crew. Only the Radio Officer could have identified him with any certainty. There has been so much confusion and so many people were injured that it wasn't possible to seal off the ship." Palfrey hitched himself up higher in his chair. "We should be able to narrow the search down, though. I want you to work with the purser — I'll arrange for him to put one of his assistants at your disposal. We must try to account for all passengers and all crew — that way we might find out the name of the assailant, we should be able to get a good description of him. You caught a glimpse, didn't you?"

"Only of his back. He was tall and dark — quite young, I should say."

"We can warn our own people, too, and might be able to use the police on this. Did you catch a glimpse of his face?"

"No."

"Julia, this could be vital — to you, and to us all. If you caught even a glimpse, you could be in danger because of it. If you caught a glimpse you could describe——"

"I didn't set eyes on his face," Julia said softly, "but I think I would recognise his back and his voice again."

6

SURPRISE

PALFREY left the S.S. *Seafarer* when Nice was really stirring. As he was driven past the harbour towards a hotel on the Promenade des Anglais, the flower and vegetable market was astir, steel-tipped shoes and boots were rattling on the cobbles, rickety old trams were clattering, cleaners were washing down

the streets and the promenade. The little bakeries were open-
ing, the scent of newly-baked bread wafted on the air, the first
of the school children in their tight short pants and short socks
moved along the pavements, carrying long, appetising looking
loaves. The sea was calm as a mill-pond, with no trace here
of the tidal wave — which had been a misnomer, of course.
There had been a fairly heavy wave on some parts of the
North African coast, and some on the French coast, but the
Riviera hadn't suffered much.

Palfrey was pondering all this when he got out of the taxi
outside the big, white hotel, where already one or two couples
were sitting on the terrace, eating croissants or *petits pains;* a
few tired-looking waiters were standing about.

Palfrey turned into the hotel.

He knew, as he had known much of his life, that he walked
with danger. He was sure that if "they" had known who Julia
and Simon were, and had tried to kill them, they knew him.
They had been fooled by Morris, if the signs were right;
Morris was the type of man who made a good agent because
so few people would suspect him. Morris apart — "they" had
known two of his agents and had tried to kill them. "They"
had also known that Corvell was on board, so they must have
been wanting him for some time.

Why want him dead?

"No," Palfrey said aloud. "That's not the right question."

He was near the reception desk. "*M'sieu?*" a clerk murmured.

"Sorry," Palfrey said. "I have arranged to have a room for
a few hours."

"Ah. Dr Palfrey?"

"Yes."

"I have it ready," the clerk said. He raised a hand for a boy
in a misty grey uniform to come up; a lad who looked as if he
should still be in bed. "Take Dr Palfrey to Suite 101."

"Yes, sir." The lad's English had only a trace of accent.

They went up smoothly in the lift, along two wide passages
into the suite. It was a huge room, with a balcony overlooking
the sea, with bedroom leading off. A faint perfume hovered,

presumably left by the previous occupant. The boy's fingers closed over a coin, he smiled, bobbed his head, dropped into French for *merci bien, m'sieu*, and went out.

Palfrey locked the door, and strolled across to the window, where the Venetian blinds were down. He raised one of them. The scene beyond was breathtakingly beautiful — and in that lovely sea, so serene and so misty a blue, death had struck savagely during the night. The first of the morning's breezes was rippling the surface in places, making a pattern on the water. It seemed as if shadows were chasing one another.

"No," he said again, "that's not the right question." He moved to the telephone but hesitated, then raised it, and gave a number in Elisabethville, Katanga. The operator took it without batting an eye. He replaced the receiver and strolled back to the window, waiting for the call. "It wasn't a question of wanting him dead. They could have killed him without serious trouble — we can't be absolutely sure we can prevent assassination." He spoke in a voice a little above a whisper. "They could have killed him as they killed the Radio Officer, and tried to kill Julia. They wouldn't start a tidal wave to *kill* one man."

He knew that, logically, he was right. So, why had they started that tidal wave? Why had they worked in such a way? Why had they been so utterly ruthless and heedless of human life? Now he was faced with questions which he could not answer, but the glimmering of a possible answer came to mind. He stood with a cigarette, unlit, between his fingers, peering out to sea, listening for the first little *ting* of the telephone to tell him that the call was through.

He did not hear a *ting*! He did hear another sound, very faint, only just audible.

He did not move his head, but listened even more intently. As he stood there, he was more aware of the perfume. A rustling sound came quite distinctly, but he could not be sure that it was in this suite; it might be out in the passage, might even be outside the window — a gaily-coloured sunblind, perhaps, stirred by the strengthening breeze.

The telephone bell blared.

He started, turned, looked across at the open doorway of the bedroom, but saw nothing. The harsh ringing sound went on and on. He stretched out his hand and took the receiver off, standing now so that he looked at the door all the time.

"M'sieu, it is your call to Elisabethville."

"Thank you."

"One moment, please."

He held on. He could discern no movement in the bedroom, and tried to persuade himself that he was wrong about the perfume, it could not have become stronger. The window shook a little, and a Venetian blind rattled. He moved so that he could see the balcony. Red, white and blue tassels of the sun blind were dancing.

"Sap," a man said in a very deep voice. "How are you?"

"Stefan," Palfrey said, almost as fervently. "I'm fine. Worried, but fine in myself."

He wished that he could turn his whole thoughts to this conversation. Stefan Andromovitch, his oldest friend and joint leader of Z5, knew a great deal about his concern over the mysterious happenings at sea. In fact only Stefan knew how great were his fears that someone had found out how to operate from the depths. Probably, too, only Stefan fully appreciated how dangerous this could be to the nations able to ride the waves, but which did not yet begin to understand the forces beneath them.

They had known each other for so long that words between them were seldom important. Whenever they met, even after a long period of separation, a firm handshake, a steady glance at each other, and then they could start to talk about work or whatever was on their minds. Deep affection as well as understanding developed over many years made them almost as close as brothers, although their backgrounds were so different. Dr Stanislaus Alexander Palfrey, whose initials gave him his nickname, came from the English aristocracy; Eton, Oxford, a medical degree. . . . Stefan Andromovitch was a Muscovite who had been indoctrinated in his early years with Stalinism, but had become one of the first Russians to doubt the need for ideological warfare. Yet he had served his masters until Moscow had seen in him the qualities needed for liaison with the West.

He had accepted the deputy leadership of Z5 with the knowledge and approval of Moscow. He was completely free — as free as Palfrey — from obligations to his government, except that he should serve Z5, which also served them.

Palfrey and Andromovitch had not met for several weeks, nor talked together for ten days, until now. Stefan had been to Elisabethville to try to resolve some problems there; his work was almost finished.

"Exactly what happened last night?" Andromovitch asked.

Very slowly, very precisely, Palfrey told him. He felt sure that Stefan must know that he was speaking with reserve, and that might puzzle the Russian. At least he was sure that he left out nothing of importance. There was no sight of movement in the bedroom, but that perfume still teased him.

"I hope to get a description of the man who attacked Julia, and killed the Radio Officer," Palfrey went on. "But I'm not yet sure. So far, that's our only clue."

"Sap, is someone with you?"

"I think so."

"*Now* I understand," Stefan said. "Are you——" alarm rose in his voice. "Are you all right? Are you in any danger?"

"I don't think that," Palfrey said carefully. In fact he believed that had someone come here to kill him, they would have tried long before this. "No, I don't think so. Have you nearly finished?"

"I can come wherever you like at any time."

"At once," said Palfrey promptly. "Here, in Nice."

"I will be with you by this time tomorrow," Andromovitch promised. His voice was back to normal; he spoke perfect English with great precision, the only indication that it was not his native tongue being the absolute perfection of his enunciation of each syllable. "Sap, listen to me."

"Yes."

"Shall I telephone Duval in Nice and make him send someone to you? He could have a man there in ten or fifteen minutes. If you even suspect danger——"

"That's a good idea," Palfrey said. "Thanks, Stefan. I'll see you tomorrow."

"Please God," Stefan Andromovitch said, and hung up.

Palfrey put down the receiver. He heard the *ting* of the bell, then the rustling of the wind at the window. When he looked out to sea, the surface was ruffled everywhere, a few white horses laced the waves. Early morning swimmers were out already, and there was more noise on the terrace and on the boulevard below.

In here, nothing moved.

Palfrey slid his right hand into his pocket and took out a cigarette-case; built in to one end was a small automatic pistol, one of the most innocent-looking of the weapons he so often needed. He put a cigarette to his lips as he went towards the bedroom door. He pushed it wider open, and dodged to one side; then he felt as foolish as he had ever done in his life.

A girl was in the big double bed, a bed of silver and gold colourings in a room of gold.

She was sitting up on her pillows, wearing a pink jacket with angora wool, or something quite as soft and delicate, pulled up beneath her chin. She had a lovely face, a lovely skin, and beautiful blue eyes; she looked a little like a doll. She smiled at him, as if delighted. The perfume was much stronger in this room.

"Good morning," she said.

Her voice had a bell-like clarity which was somehow not quite real. Something about her reminded Palfrey of a Japanese girl, although her features were certainly not Japanese. The only word that sprang to mind about her was "demure". Here she was, in the bed in his room, sitting up as if she were waiting for her husband on their wedding night — *demure*! He found himself tempted to laugh; something about her caused that impulse.

"Hallo," he said. "How are you?"

"I am very well, thank you."

Her arms, bare from halfway between elbow and wrist, rested on the golden-coloured bedspread; nicely rounded little arms, too. She wasn't much more than a child, he thought — and that "I am very well, thank you" seemed almost like a child's recitation of a well-learned phrase. Palfrey went to the side of the bed, and sat down, staring at her. She watched him eagerly, or hopefully? *Invitingly?*

"Who are you?" he asked.

"Who would you like me to be?"

"Who would——" he began, then stopped again. He could not prevent himself from smiling. Her lips twitched at the corners, as if she knew exactly what he was thinking, and also appreciated the joke.

It was like playing a game with a child.

Palfrey needed a little time to recover from the surprise, to weigh up the situation and decide what best to do — and the obvious thing was to play this game.

"I don't really know," he said. "I think perhaps I would like you to be my daughter."

"*Daughter!*" she echoed. And she leaned forward.

It was no accident, he was sure, that as she did so the bed jacket fell apart. He could not fail to see the smooth, white, curving beauty of her breasts. It was quite intentional, and it made nonsense of the notion that she was a child; small she might be, but undoubtedly a mature woman. She made no other effort to entice him, except to raise her hands a little; when she put them down again, the jacket fell into position, but left more than enough for him to see. His gaze, drawn for a moment, shifted to her face. She was laughing at him.

"You did ask me who I'd like you to be," he reminded her.

"Must I still be your *daughter*?"

"I think now that I'm glad you're not."

She had beautifully marked, near-black eyebrows, and with her jet black hair, that explained the impression that she was like a Japanese. Her eyes were sparkling, too, as if she was laughing at him in real fun.

"You would not like a daughter of yours to be in a strange man's bed, perhaps."

"No," Palfrey said. "I would not."

"You are very old-fashioned."

"That I can believe."

"In *every* way."

For the first time since he had seen her, he began to think and probe for reasons for her presence. One thing was glaringly obvious; this had something to do with "them", but he had not yet given that serious thought. His own neglect to do so puzzled him. It was almost as if he were satisfied to sit on the side of the bed and talk to the girl with this rather avuncular solemnity.

In every way, she had said, he was old-fashioned. What ways? In his attitude towards her? In what he was doing? In his attitude towards Corvell?

"What other ways?" he asked.

"Dr Palfrey." She leaned forward again, thrusting her hands towards him. "You are a very lonely man. You must have been ever since you lost your wife. I have been told much about you. A man should not spend all his time alone — that is *very* old-fashioned."

"A man must spend his time as he wants to."

"Is that what you do? Or do you spend your time as olden day convention — romantic convention, perhaps — says you should?" Her voice was very matter of fact, as she leaned still nearer, the jacket gaping more. He had not been so close to a woman since he had last been with Drusilla. He was acutely conscious of desire, and he sensed that she was here simply to create such desire, to seduce him from the work he had to do.

"Dr Palfrey," she said, and then more softly: "Sap." How had she come to know that nickname? How had she come to know so much — *how had she come to know that he would be here?* "Sap," she went on, "why are you wasting your life? Why are you throwing everything worth living for away? Why are you

trying to save the old world, all the old archaic wasteful ways
of life? Why don't you cut yourself free from the past — your
own past and the world's? Why don't you come and help to
make the future?"

7

INVITATION . . .

PALFREY moved back a little, away from the woman, but
stayed on the bed. Again she rested her hands on the bedspread, and again the fluffy edges of the jacket half concealed
and yet revealed the beauty she was offering. Palfrey felt quite
composed, quite sure of himself, and yet his mind was not
working as quickly as he wished, and as it usually did; she
had slowed down his reactions. That was hardly surprising.
He smiled at the reflection. She gave a quick answering smile,
making him realise how easy it was to see the funny side with
her. The funny side of *what*? Was this situation so funny? How
was it he could sit here and talk with her and jest with her —
while the Radio Officer was cold in his coffin, Simon Alting
was seriously ill in hospital, Julia was in danger — or had
been — in grave danger, and many innocent people had died,
Corvell perhaps among them?

Why didn't he feel agitated? Or angry? Why wasn't he
concentrating on the need to twist this situation to the best
possible use? What made him so calm? — or was the word
complacent?

"Did you hear me?" she asked. "Why don't you come and
help to make the future?"

"I am helping to make it."

"You may think so, but all you are really doing is rebuilding
the old world on top of the dying one. You're too good for that,
Sap; you're much too good."

"Where is this new world of yours?"

He had an absurd notion that she would begin to talk about

life on another planet; absurd, because he knew what conditions were like on the planets which had so far been discovered
by man, and knew also that life was virtually impossible on
them. But when she said "new world" she gave the impression
that she was really talking of a different place from earth.

He must stand up; must move away from her.

She leaned forward again and for the first time took his
hands; hers were cool and very soft, but she held him more
firmly than he had expected.

"Sap," she whispered, "it can be wonderful, so very wonderful down with us. And you are one of the men we need most."

Down with us. This was the first indication she had given
that the world she came from was below the earth — or below
the sea. For the first time he realised that the bed jacket was
filmy and almost like the skin of a delicately coloured fish;
there was a gossamer beauty about it, about her, almost as if
he were seeing her through faintly iridescent water.

Down with us.

"So this is an offer," Palfrey said. He freed himself and stood
up. She lay back on the pillows, smiling serenely, as if his
attitude amused her. He had a strange feeling, that she was
older and wiser than he, in spite of her youthfulness.

"Yes," she said. "It is a very serious offer, and you would
be most unwise to refuse it."

"Just where do you want me to come?"

She did not answer at first. He thought the serenity of her
smile lessened, as if something had annoyed her. When she did
speak, it was almost sharply.

"You will find out soon enough."

"Exactly what do you want me to do?" he asked next.

Now that he was further away from her, his mind worked
more freely; it was as if closeness to her beauty exerted a kind
of thraldom which a distance even of a few feet could break.
He stood with his back to the window, studying her; and he
told himself that he had never seen a woman or child who
looked so — blemishless. Every part of her that he could see
was free from physical blemish.

"If you want to know more," she said, "you must come and talk with the Patriarch."

"Who is the Patriarch?"

"Sap," she said softly, "there isn't a chance, not a single, solitary chance, of you learning anything from me by sudden questions, trick questions, or subterfuge of any kind. There is absolutely no chance at all. We have ways of making sure that we cannot be compelled to talk. Some of our men, our agents, come to the Upper World to carry out special missions. We had two agents on the *Seafarer*, one now dead, one alive, and two in Nice. Others can be summoned quickly. Usually they return with their mission accomplished," she went on. "Occasionally they fail. Some, who are injured so that they can never return to us, kill themselves. One did, here in the South of France. He escaped from the ship — the *Seafarer* — after killing the Radio Officer and attempting to prevent the woman Julia from reporting to you. He broke his arm in an accident. That impaired his physical perfection. He passed on a message to another of our agents, and killed himself. I was told of this before I came here. When I arrived here, I posed as a maid, which is very easy — but everything in the Upper World is easy to us, if we desire it sufficiently."

Palfrey thought: "*Upper World?*"

He said: "Why was it necessary to kill——"

"Sap," she interrupted, "life and death in your sense has no importance to us — death is the means to an end. Only a very few are indispensable. It is necessary to make sure none of our agents is caught. It is also necessary to show how ruthless we can be. Don't try to adhere to your own standards. It will get you nowhere. There is no way in which you can find out who the Patriarch is, nor where I come from, nor what he is doing — unless you do what I tell you to, and go where I tell you. I can promise you this: there is a new kind of wonder, a new concept of life, a state of exaltation and of ecstasy easily available to you. It is available to anyone who is invited, and to anyone who helps to make this new world. If we didn't want you, I would not be here."

"You would not be offering yourself," Palfrey said, sharply, "with the Patriarch's connivance——"

She laughed again; whether she intended to or not, she made him feel a little foolish.

"Oh, Sap, you are *too* old-fashioned to be true. I told you not to use the archaic standards you are used to. What is relationship between the sexes if it is not to help to create new worlds, new people, new concepts — what is there wrong about a physically perfect man with a fine mind mating with a physically perfect woman with — shall I say a *good* mind?"

"Is modesty old-fashioned, too?" asked Palfrey drily.

"I have to try to meet you halfway," she said. "Sap, while you work for the governments of the dying world you are wasting your time, throwing away wonderful opportunities. I am offering you one to break from it all. You will never regret taking it, I can promise you that. We need you. We need all men of ideals, men with clear minds, men who know exactly what they want and where they are going. Sap——"

He stood, quite still, watching her.

She thrust the jacket off her shoulders with a swift shrug. She pushed the bedclothes back, and, with another quick movement, got out of bed. She was breathtakingly beautiful. Flawless — *without blemish*. His heart began to beat suffocatingly fast, he felt it difficult to breathe.

"Sap." She stepped towards him with her arms outstretched. "Why don't you let me show you what this new world can be like? I promise you that it will be something more wonderful, more ecstatic, than anything you've known before. No woman could ever give you what I can give."

It was a strange, almost a frightening moment. He felt as if she were actually touching him and he could not move away, but would have to surrender. His thoughts were in turmoil; thoughts no longer of Julia Shawn, the ship, Corvell, Stefan Andromovitch, but just of this woman and her promise and her beauty, her talk of the new world divorced from all the old — the old world that he had lost with Drusilla, the old world which——

Drusilla.

"*No woman could ever give you what I can give you,*" this woman had said.

Drusilla's face seemed to hover in front of Palfrey. Drusilla, tall, in her way so very lovely. And his, loving him until she had died as he had loved her; and as he still loved her memory. No woman could give what Drusilla had given him.

"Sap!" this woman cried. She was just in front of him, touching him; her eyes were huge and pleading, as if she sensed that she was about to lose him. "Sap, come with me. Let me convince you——"

Instead of backing away, he closed with her, put his arms round her, held her tight, and then hoisted her off her feet. She seemed too startled to shout or to move. He carried her over to the bed as if he were going to surrender to her seductive body. Then he flipped a sheet off, and rolled her in it. There was a flurry of pink and white legs, arms, body — next moment she was like a cocoon, with only her head showing at the top and her feet at the bottom. He picked up another sheet, and repeated the swaddling, so that she looked like a huge white cotton bobbin, fat in the middle and tapering down to head and to feet. She had still not recovered from the shock. When he stood back, leaving her facing him, her mouth was open and she was gasping for breath, and her eyes looked huge.

"Now let's have a little talk," he said. "I feel safer when you're like that." He grinned at her. "Who are you?"

She didn't answer.

"You may think you're proof against persuasion," Palfrey said, and a grimmer note deepened in his voice, "but you'll find out that you're not. The old world has its methods of persuasion, you know — successful ones, too. We have perfected a brain-washing technique which will do in an hour what used to take months. Drugs are the secret. The drugs break down all forms of resistance. We add a little physical roughness and some mental pressure for good measure, but the real secret is in the drugs. It's much better to talk freely without the drugs, but if necessary I can administer them."

He turned to his dressing-table, picked up a small toilet case, opened it, and drew out a bright, chromium cylinder. He unscrewed the cap from this and pulled out a hypodermic syringe. He put this down, where the woman could see it, then unclipped an ampoule of the truth drug from the cylinder.

He picked up the hypodermic, and turned to face the woman.

Her eyes seemed to be closing, as if she were suddenly overwhelmingly tired.

"That won't help you!" he said in sudden alarm. "Feigning sleep won't be any good."

She opened her eyes again. He was reminded vividly of the days when his own son had been very young, six or seven perhaps, and had wanted desperately to stay up late. He had been allowed to, as a great treat. After a while, tiredness had overtaken him. Excitement, enjoyment, the thrill of staying up were all set at naught. His eyes had begun to droop, had closed, opened again, closed, opened, closed . . .

He had fallen asleep, with music going and games being played and everything he wanted to eat and drink within reach. Palfrey had carried him up to his bedroom, Drusilla had left the guests for a few minutes to come and settle him down for the night. That was the kind of oneness there had been in their family.

This girl was asleep.

"I tell you to wake up!" Palfrey exclaimed, and he pinched her ear.

She did not stir.

"*Wake up!*" he ordered, and nipped her nostrils and held them for a moment, to try to frighten her into thinking that she could not breathe.

She slept on.

His own breathing was coming short and sharp when at last he stood back from her. Her eyelashes, black as her hair and eyebrows, swept the peach-bloom cheeks; there was no change in her beauty, but she had been able to induce this "sleep" at will. Sleep? Or coma? He knew of strange behaviour and strange mind control — in yogis, in religious fanatics, in men who had trained themselves all their lives to the conquest of mind over matter — but he had never seen anything like this.

*   *   *

Palfrey tried the old methods; jabbing pins into the soles of her feet; pulling her hair; tweaking her ears again. She did not stir.

He was a physician, but had not practised for many years, and he had no equipment here. He left the woman on the bed and went to the telephone and called Duval, who answered in person.

"Do you need help, Dr Palfrey? Andromovitch telephoned from Elisabethville to say you were in some alarm."

"I need a doctor who can be trusted absolutely," Palfrey replied. "How quickly can you send one here?"

"What is it for?"

"For someone who appears to be in a coma due to hypnosis."

"You need a specialist," Duval said. His English was as good as Andromovitch's, for he had spent much of his youth and many of the war years in England. "There is a Dr Phillippe Gaston, at the hospital. He is well known for his experiments in the hypnotic treatment of physical conditions. *Coma*, Dr Palfrey? Who is it?"

"I don't yet know. Dr Gaston won't know, either. I want him to come simply to examine the patient and to give me a diagnosis and an opinion, then to forget the whole affair."

"I will arrange it," Duval promised. Then he said anxiously: "Is there any danger for you?"

"No physical danger," Palfrey assured him. "Not yet, anyhow."

"There are two men on the promenade, opposite your room; you have only to shout for them. Two electricians are

in the hotel, on the second floor near your room. You need
only call for them. If you want more——"

"Just Dr Gaston," Palfrey said. "Oh — and ask him to
bring a flashlight camera."

"I will. Dr Palfrey——"

"Yes?"

"You sound so — remote."

Palfrey said in a more natural voice: "I've had a bit of a
shock, and I'm afraid it shows through. I'm all right."

"I hope you will still be all right when I tell you that the
man who killed the Radio Officer on board the *Seafarer* has
been found," Duval said. "Either he shot himself or he was
killed. His body was found in one of the valleys in the mountains, badly bruised and with one arm broken."

Palfrey exclaimed: "*Dead*," in a shocked voice.

"I am afraid so," said Duval. "If you need me again,
telephone and I will be here."

Palfrey said: "I'm sure you will. Thank you, Duval."

He rang off.

The breeze was still stirring the blind, but did not seem so
strong as it had been, or else he was used to the noise. He kept
thinking of the man who had been on board the liner; who
had been given the task of stopping Julia from reporting what
she had seen, who had killed the Radio Officer, and who in
turn was dead. That man had been the most likely way of
tracing the source of the attacks. Now the only hope was
through this woman on the bed.

She was the only hope, remember. Yet she had come of her
own free will, expecting to find him here, supremely confident
of her power over him, although he had decided to come
ashore only a few hours ago. Very few people had known
that.

It wasn't true, he reminded himself. Several people had
known, and one might have talked — members of the crew or
of the passengers. The woman had not needed second sight to
anticipate his presence here, but she had needed to be very
quick.

She and the agents she talked of must have been in Nice, so it should not be too difficult to identify her or to trace her leader.

He wasn't convinced, even as he told himself that.

He sat down, wrote out a description of the woman, checked, and made sure that it was as accurate as he could get it. Then he telephoned Merritt in London, and dictated it to him. Merritt would relay it to Nice, to Paris, and to all Z5 agents everywhere.

"The lassie sounds quite a belle," Merritt conceded. "I'll get this out to all our people and to all police forces, Sap. You want to know from anyone who's seen her — anyone, anywhere. Is that right?"

"Especially from anyone who knows where she lives, or knows her family."

"I'll do everything I can," Merritt promised.

Palfrey knew that he would do more; working through Z5 and through New Scotland Yard, through *Interpol* and other international police organisations, he would do everything that could be done to trace this woman.

Woman? Or girl?

How was it that she seemed to combine youth with age, and simplicity with maturity?

As the thought passed through his mind, there was a tap at the door. Duval's two men would not allow anyone who was unauthorised to come, but Palfrey opened the door carefully, ready to dodge to one side.

The man outside was tall, very thin, middle-aged, somehow very French. He carried a doctor's black bag in one hand and a camera in the other.

"M'sieu?" He gave a quick, mechanical smile. "I am Dr Gaston. You are expecting me, I believe."

8

COMA

"It is certainly very remarkable," Dr Gaston said. He stood back from the bed, where the girl–woman lay, and pulled the sheet up from her knees to her chin. He stood back, a hand at his own chin, frowning. Palfrey had already discovered that he was inclined to strike attitudes — to frown, clap his hands together, lean back with his head on one side, purse his lips and mumble to himself; but everything Palfrey saw of the way the man worked suggested that he knew his job.

He began to toy with the stethoscope dangling from his neck.

"Undoubtedly, coma — but for what reason? It is not alcoholic. It is not *encephalitis lethargica* — you say you have seen no sign of waking when you have called and shouted at her? Nor have I. I see nothing to suggest any cerebral thrombosis indication or any virus disease, and the onset of the condition was too sudden to allow for such a diagnosis, whatever the other signs. I do not know enough of her history to suggest a cerebral vascular lesion."

He stood back from the bed and stared at Palfrey. He thrust his bony chin forward, and rubbed his hands.

"M'sieu!"

"Have you come to any conclusion?" asked Palfrey, patiently.

"I have formed an opinion which I would not wish to state in evidence without much more knowledge of the patient's history, and further acquaintance with other outside factors. I have come across a form of it several times in the past. I think it could best be called a hypnotic trance, in this case self-induced. It has been most common in Eastern countries, particularly in India, the Sudan and in parts of Persia. But this comes as no surprise to you, Dr Palfrey, of that I am sure."

Palfrey said: "I didn't want to believe it."

"Come, come! As a medical man, and a man with such an intellect——" Gaston struck a smiling pose, hands raised, fingers spread. "You must believe what your eyes and your mind tell you. Please——" he seemed eager. "You agree with me?"

"Hypnotic trance or coma, probably self-induced," Palfrey agreed. Could the ability to withdraw herself from the conscious world explain the girl–woman's absolute confidence that he could not make her talk? He began to wonder how long she would be in the coma, but he did not have to wonder what he must do.

"So," Dr Gaston said. "Do you wish me to arrange for her to go to a hospital?"

Palfrey's eyes were drooping. It was a long time before he answered: "Yes. Yes, please. That would be best."

"I shall watch her myself whenever I can," Gaston declared. "The moment she shows any sign of coming out of the coma, I shall send for you."

"Good," Palfrey said. "Here, please."

"Of course," said the doctor.

He put his stethoscope, his blood-pressure equipment and other instruments away, and stalked to the door. His bony fingers crushed Palfrey's. "Most interesting," he declared. "*Most* interesting. Thank you for giving me the opportunity to see the patient."

He went out.

Palfrey closed the door, bolted it, and went into the bedroom. The girl had not stirred. He found her clothes on a chair near the wardrobe, but made no attempt to put them onto her; instead, he called Duval again. He was so used to finding help at hand, often in times of dire emergency, that when Duval was a long time answering he was puzzled, and soon anxious.

"Duval." The Frenchman spoke at last.

"Two things, very quickly," Palfrey said. "I want a dark-haired girl who will take risks, and——" he broke off, thinking suddenly of Julia, and had to make himself go on: "Very grave risks. I've just had an idea. Have you talked to Julia Shawn today?"

"No."

"I'll talk to her," Palfrey decided. "Now pay very close attention, will you? First — delay the ambulance that Dr Gaston is to send here for an hour, and have your own men in it."

"Yes."

"Second — instruct the two men in the hotel here to bring me a big laundry basket, and to be ready to collect it whenever I ask. They are to take it to the *Seafarer* — to Julia Shawn's cabin."

"Very well."

"And make absolutely sure it is safe when there," Palfrey said.

"What will be in it?"

Palfrey said: "A human being."

"So! Are we to release the prisoner?"

"Not until later today," Palfrey answered. "I'll see to it."

"Very good," Duval said again.

Palfrey put the receiver down, but almost at once put in a call to the ship. There was a possibility that the line was tapped, but Duval would have checked that. It was impossible to be absolutely sure that every eventuality was guarded against. He had to take risks, considered risks, such as sending the unknown woman to the ship. Surely that would be the last place that her fellow agents from "down below" would expect him to send her.

The call was a long time coming through. Before it, he came up, startled, against the realisation that he was completely himself again; his mind worked as he had trained it to. It was easy to reach decisions, and once reached, they seemed obviously the right ones. Duval's implicit obedience was a great help, but some other factor had caused this rebirth of self-confidence.

Or had the girl–woman whose name he did not know, taken confidence away while she had been with him?

The ship's exchange answered, and in a moment Julia said:

"Who is that?"

Palfrey recalled her as she had been when he had last seen her; badly frightened but trying hard not to show it — not really convinced that he was right, and that the immediate danger for her was past. Well, it had been; but now he was about to toss her back into danger, perhaps into a greater peril than she had yet known.

He said: "This is Sap."

"Why, hallo."

"Julia," he said, and hesitated. His right hand was at those strands of hair again. "Julia, I've a very tricky, sticky job for you. Much, much worse than looking after Corvell. I've been trying to think of someone else I could send, but it has to be someone naturally dark-haired, and someone who is free now. At this moment."

"I'm free," Julia said.

"If you would prefer not to——"

Her voice became more brisk. "Don't be silly, Sap. When I joined you, I knew that I wouldn't be able to count the risks. Faithful unto death, in fact. What is it you want me to do?"

That was Julia Shawn's special kind of courage.

"I had a visitor at the hotel," Palfrey told her. "I've taken her captive. They" — he paused, to give her time to grasp the significance of that "they" — then added: "think she will be in an ambulance on the way to hospital. I want you to be in that ambulance, in her place. With luck, they'll take you where they would have taken her. With luck, they might want to exchange prisoners."

"When do you want me to start?" asked Julia.

After a pause, Palfrey said: "Come here right away, will you?" His voice was husky, Julia probably had the greater composure in that moment. "You won't need to pack anything."

*　　*　　*

Julia put down the receiver and stood touching it while looking out of the closed porthole. She was on the starboard side of the ship, alongside one of the quays of the harbour. She could hear cranes and winches grinding and groaning, and just make out the tops of the heads of dockers and others on the docks. She took a quick step or two forward, and studied herself in the tall mirror of her dressing-table. She was much more pale than usual, and her eyes were almost luminously bright.

She opened a large, brown crocodile leather handbag, put in a few more make-up oddments than she would usually carry, two freshly ironed handkerchiefs and two bars of plain chocolate. She snapped the bag to, and went out. She smiled at the round-faced sergeant-at-arms standing in the passage, and he grinned back happily. Another sergeant-at-arms, tall, huge, was at the foot of the gangway. Julia walked towards him, not knowing what a picture she made in her pencil slim yellow dress with the bolero coat, pale green shoes, pale green cotton gloves. The sergeant-at-arms here towered over her.

"'Morning, miss. They got the devil, then."

"What devil?" asked Julia. She had been thinking only of this new assignment, and what it might mean.

"Why, the swine who shot Mr Green." Green was the Radio Officer. "He jumped off a precipice up in the Alpes Maritimes." He pronounced that "Alpes maritymes". "That's got rid of a bit of no good."

"Yes," Julia said. "That's fine."

As she passed him, she felt the blood recede even further from her cheeks.

A car from Duval was waiting outside the Customs shed, where a Customs officer took one look at her handbag and waved her through. She sat back in the small red Renault, thinking of the past more than of the future. Her father had served Z5; so had her lover. Her *beloved*. When they had both died in the same struggle, she had sworn that she would serve Z5 whatever the cost and whatever the risk. There were two degrees of service in Palfrey's agents; those who would take every risk, those who took limited ones. *Until death do us part*, she found herself thinking again.

Slowly, her thoughts veered towards Palfrey. She had known him for a long time, now. Socially, they were equals. He knew all about her past, the fact that she and Guy had lived together for a long time, because his wife had been "sick"; in fact, because she had been mad. She had almost forgotten that she had never been Guy's wife. Palfrey knew everything about her, then — as he seemed to about all the agents. She did not think she had ever known a man who had one tenth of the knowledge that Palfrey had — unless it was the Russian giant, Andromovitch, whom she did not know so well.

She was not in love with Palfrey, but had a deep affection for and a great faith in him. She might be frightened — she was, now — but if Palfrey thought the risk necessary, then she would take it without hesitation, although she sensed how heavy-hearted he had been when he had asked her to take the job.

She was to be kidnapped, of course, in mistake for this other woman.

She wished there were time for her to learn more about the other woman, more about what was happening. When she reached the hotel, going in by an annexe so as not to be noticed by so many people, she was whisked up to the second floor by a service lift. Palfrey welcomed her at his room door. As she stepped inside, he began to tell her what had happened, and what she was to do. In his unhurried voice he contrived to make her feel the sense of urgency. While he talked, she slipped out of her clothes into a dressing gown, ready for the ambulance. Before the ambulance men arrived, Palfrey took her into the bedroom, and they stood looking down together at the "sleeping" woman.

Julia caught her breath.

"There isn't a flaw in her skin," she almost gasped.

"Not a flaw anywhere," Palfrey agreed. "She's almost too good to be true."

"Who is she?"

"I don't know."

Julia made herself look straight into his eyes.

"There isn't much you do know about this affair, Sap, is there?"

"Far too little," he admitted. "And most of what we know you've told us. I've been trying to put myself in their position. If I've guessed right, they'll take you prisoner. They'll stop the ambulance between here and the docks, and kidnap the patient, thinking it's her." He did not look down at the girl–woman. "They may not find out their mistake for a long time. I think when they do, they'll be anxious to make sure no harm comes to her. I think they'll want an exchange."

Julia could not stop herself from saying: "They didn't worry about the man who killed the Radio Officer."

"I can only hope she is more important to them," Palfrey said. "Julia, from the moment they take you from that ambulance, keep your eyes and your ears wide open, keep all your senses alert. A word, whisper, a momentary glimpse of a face, a hand, a building, a car — any one of these things might help us to succeed in our investigation. But you know that."

"I know it," Julia said.

Then the telephone bell rang; the ambulance was waiting.

9

AMBULANCE

JULIA felt herself lifted on the stretcher, by two diminutive ambulance men. She kept her eyes closed, but the morning sunlight was bright upon them. She was bandaged about the head so that only her dark hair showed, and about the face, so that it would be difficult for anyone to recognise her at first glance; those who knew her well would recognise her only if they were able to concentrate. She felt herself pushed into position in the ambulance; the hot sunlight was cut off, and that brought relief. The doors closed. One ambulance man

was squatting on a bucket seat opposite her; she sensed that
he was staring. The engine started. She felt the slight tremor
of the vehicle, before it began to move away slowly, then
gradually it gathered speed. The springing was remarkable —
she felt a slight swaying motion, that was all.

How soon would it happen?

She told herself suddenly that it might never happen, that
Palfrey might be wrong. Should she pray that he was right or
wrong? She felt an almost overwhelming temptation to open
her eyes, but resisted it. The ambulance turned a corner. As
it did so, she felt the ambulance attendant touch her bare arm.
She opened her eyes now, saw him leaning forward, saw the
glittering of a hypodermic syringe in his hand.

"It is Dr Palfrey's order," he said.

He plunged the needle into her flesh.

She thought, near panic: *Sap, Sap, why didn't you warn me?*
She tried to sit up, but then dropped back on her pillows again.

"It will make you sleep," the ambulance man said
soothingly.

It would make her sleep, so that she would not know what
was happening to her; and she might never know life again.
Sap, Sap, Sap, why did you do it? She knew why he had, of
course; knew that if she had known that she was to be unconscious when she was "captured" it would have been far
worse for her to make the decision to go peacefully — it would
have been intolerable. Palfrey must have hated the deception
even more than telling her what he wanted of her — Sap, she
thought, why didn't you do it yourself? Why didn't you come
with me?

She felt a darkness descend upon her, and sank into the
void beyond.

*   *   *

The ambulance took the back streets which led to the hospital. The driver was one of Duval's men, and so was the
attendant inside; each of them knew what to expect. The
driver turned a corner towards Juan les Pins, into a short,

straight road, and saw an antiquated black Renault parked on
one side, a small, smart red Fiat almost straight in front of the
ambulance; there was no room to pass. As the ambulance
slowed down, a man stepped towards the driver briskly,
smiled up — and showed the automatic pistol in his right hand.

"You will come down," he ordered.

The driver said: "Come down? What are you thinking
about? I've a patient in here, she's got to be rushed to
hospital."

"You will come down. . . ." the man insisted.

*   *   *

In the room at the hotel, Palfrey was taking reports which
had come in from Merritt already. So far there was none of
anyone like the "girl–woman", but it was much too early for
those. There were some which might well have a great significance. Between moments of wondering what was happening
to Julia Shawn, Palfrey forced himself to study these. It was
an almost shattering revelation in one way — *if* in fact it was
a revelation and not coincidence. He had learned to accept
coincidences as normal, but this one — or rather, these six —
was unbelievable.

There had been the seven exceptional waves, some appar-
ently tidal, with restricted effects, in various parts of the world.

> The Pacific, near Hawaii
> The Pacific, near Perth, Australia
> The Indian Ocean — near the Seychelles
> The Red Sea, near Aden
> The Atlantic, off the Outer Hebrides
> The North Sea, off the Irish Coast
> The Mediterranean — near here.

The reports of the effects of the waves were the same in
every case — no seismograph indication, no natural cause as
far as it was known, no recorded earth shock of any kind — all
had been due, as far as anyone could tell, to some kind of local
undersea eruption, or possibly to a hurricane which had blown

itself out quickly. Palfrey, who had seen the reports before and asked in each case for further information, had not seen them together in this way. Nor had he seen the connection with the disappearances of men such as Corvell.

He saw it now.

At or close to the nearest coastal area affected by each wave, a research physicist, a chemist or a mathematical genius had been staying; and from those coastal areas, the men had disappeared.

Palfrey had found himself pondering about the waves before, but freak waves were not unusual, and there had been no reason to connect the disappearances with the waves. Now that he studied the disappearances together, and knew what had happened with the *Seafarer*, the coincidence was almost beyond belief. Seven prominent scientists had vanished, and there was almost certainly some connection between their disappearances and the waves.

Palfrey studied a small chart, prepared in simple outline, showing the Mercator projection of the world, and the places from which the men had disappeared and the areas of the waves — and he did not doubt that these were connected.

He began to put in names, opposite the places where the coastal areas had been affected, and also to make a list of everything noted on the red spots on the chart.

The list read:

1. Dr Fumagi Kyma, American marine bacteriologist, specialist in bacterial and virus diseases known to or believed to originate from oceans, known to be near a break-through in cancer research — had been tunny fishing near Hawaii while on vacation. His ship had foundered and the body of his skipper had been found. He had been presumed dead.

2. Professor Herbert Rackley, Australian research physicist, believed to have made discoveries of radio-active properties off parts of the great Barrier Reef, surf-riding on West Australian beaches — reported drowned and pulled under by sharks.

3. Dr Sigismund Dahl, Swedish specialist in heart diseases, the man most famous for the artificial or plastic heart which it was believed would soon be commonly used in certain cases of heart disease and might extend life by many years when heart disease and/or weakness was the cause of ill-health — lost on an exploration cruise near the Seychelles.

4. Dr John Smith, English specialist in electronic devices, believed to be nearer to making a computer which could think than anyone else alive — staying at the British base near Aden while making atmospheric and heat tests of a small computer for measuring pressures at various depths of water — believed lost with his companions when on a small yacht.

5. Mr Otto Schumacher, marine engineer, one of the leading specialists on submarine travel, known to have been experimenting on single-person submarines which would enable individuals to go under water for several thousand miles without surfacing. He had been caught in a storm off the Outer Hebrides, and been presumed lost with all on board the ship in which he had been working.

6. Patrick Mullahy, the Irish scientist who specialised in high tensile steel, and in metallurgical work including that on submarines. He was responsible for heat resisting alloys which enabled submarines to stay under water for exceptionally long periods. He had been lost while fishing off Dublin.

7. Corvell.

When he had finished this, Palfrey studied the list and began to see more in common among them. All had been fairly near the coast, near coastal areas which had been affected by the freak waves, which he now realised might have been underwater disturbances caused by the silver midget submarines, or whatever Julia had seen. There was a pattern, too. Each man had been a specialist in his own particular sphere; each had been probably the greatest expert in his field.

The first disappearance had happened over eighteen months

ago, and the others had followed at fairly regular three
monthly intervals, attracting less attention than they would
had they all happened within a few weeks. The fact that the
first disappearance was so long ago alarmed Palfrey now, for
it meant that "they" had been operating for a long time. None
of Z5's agents in any part of the world had reported any
indication of "them"; had he not taken such extreme care
with Corvell, Palfrey might have known nothing even now.

The telephone bell rang.

He turned towards it, glancing at his watch. It was now
half past ten, and Julia had been gone for nearly an hour.
Every minute of the last half hour he had been expecting a
report. Was this it?

He stretched out his hand for the receiver, and looked into
the bedroom as he did so. There was no movement there; as
far as he knew the girl–woman had been in that coma all the
time. The windows were bolted and the shutters closed, it was
impossible for anyone to get in or out of the bedroom except
through this outer room.

"Palfrey."

"Dr Palfrey," Duval said. "You were right."

Palfrey swallowed a lump in his throat.

"Just what happened?"

"The ambulance was held up halfway between the hotel
and the hospital. The attendants were taken in a small car and
stranded on the mountains — they have just telephoned me.
The ambulance was taken into a cul-de-sac on the mountain
road. When discovered, it was empty."

"Empty," echoed Palfrey.

"She was not there," Duval told him. "Already we have
searched the area around, and there is no sign of her. Undoubtedly she was taken away."

"I see," said Palfrey. His mouth felt dry. "The first part's
gone according to plan, anyhow. Thanks, Duval."

"All the police, all my agents and the coastal authorities
have been alerted," Duval assured him. "If there should be
any sign of SKJ you will be told at once."

"Thanks," Palfrey said.

"Do you need anything more?"

"Not now." Palfrey forced some warmth into his voice. "Not yet, anyhow. But when I do want it, I know you'll give it to me."

"You are very kind." There was a note of gratification in Duval's voice, and Palfrey rang off wondering whether he should have given Duval a meed of praise earlier; it was so easy to take first-class work for granted. It was easy, too, to take the organisation of Z5 for granted — at one time, when it had started, there had been an agent here, an agent there, but vast areas of the civilised world had not been covered. Now it was like a world police force; a world secret police force.

At least he hadn't taken Julia Shawn for granted.

He spent another five minutes studying the reports and the charts, and then went into the other room. The girl–woman lay there, just as she had after Dr Gaston had examined her; she had not stirred. Her breathing was very soft, shallow and hardly perceptible, her pulse rate low but not dangerously so. He placed his thumb on her right eyelid, and raised it; she stared up at him, unseeing. He did the same with the other, and the result was repeated. He moved further back from the bed and stared at her.

A hypnotic coma — *self*-imposed?

It was possible for some forms of hypnosis to be effective at a distance; with the hypnotists in the next room, perhaps, or in the next street. Victims, often called "patients", had been known to "sleep" for days on end. But there was nothing to suggest that anyone else had worked on her mind. If it was self-imposed, when would she come out of it?

Was there any way to bring her out?

A hypnotic trance could be highly dangerous, and he did not want her dead; in fact the very last thing he wanted was to lose her. He put his hands on the foot panel of the bed and stared at her, remembering how she had made it easy for him to laugh, how pleasant it had been when she had been awake.

The odd thing was that he had not been greatly affected by the seduction scene — looking back, it amused him. But there was nothing to be amused about. In this woman's mind, so comatose at this moment, were all the secrets he wanted to know. He must not risk damaging it.

He moved again, wrapped her up in a sheet, lifted her off the bed, and carried her to the big wicker laundry basket which Duval's men had brought in. There was a pillow at the bottom. He placed her in it, carefully. Laying her on her side, with her knees bent a little, there was good room for her; she was almost tiny; almost. He had not seen her profile so clearly before, and now he looked at it intently; flawless, of course — the contours of the cheeks, the outline of the eyebrows, the shape of the nose; that was what Julia had first noticed.

He put two pillows on top of her, leaving her head clear, then closed the box. The lid just pressed the pillows down. He went to the door, and called one of the "electricians", who came at once. His companion followed. They took the laundry basket out of the room, and began to follow their precise instructions, already given.

When they had gone, Palfrey went back into the suite. From this moment until he knew that the girl–woman was safe in Julia's cabin, he would be on edge. The impersonation might have been discovered by now, of course, the hotel might be closely watched; *he* would probably be closely watched. The great impulse was to go after the men and accompany the laundry basket, but that would be folly; he must not show any particular interest in it.

He put the papers away in a brief-case, and was ready to go. He hesitated, stripped, had a cool shower, and dressed, picked up the brief-case, and went out.

No one appeared to take any interest in him.

A quartette — piano, two violins and a 'cello — was playing on the hotel terrace, where twenty or thirty people sat drinking coffee, having a late *petit déjeuner*, or sipping the first *apéritif* of the day. He waited for a stream of traffic to pass, then stepped across the boulevard, pausing for a moment between the huge palm trees. The deck chairs were filling up, the fat old women in their drab grey uniforms were collecting the money for them, the bells on the ticket machines kept going *ting-ting-ting*. The beaches were crowded at every bathing station. The sun-bathers were stretched out, near-naked, sun-tan lotion glistening on pink bodies, pale bodies, golden-brown bodies, near-black bodies. No one took any notice. Children were screaming and jumping about at the water's edge. Palfrey walked towards the market and the harbour. He was hatless, and the sun was hot on his head. Now and again he toyed with a few tendrils of hair, then patted them down. Occasionally, he paused, leaned against the railings, and appeared to gaze idly at the beach and the reclining bodies; actually he was looking ahead and behind him. There was still nothing to indicate that he had been followed.

He walked on.

No one among these crowds could even begin to guess the anxieties on his mind — and no one, looking at him, would have suspected that any existed. He was smiling faintly. He walked with deceptive leisureliness, actually covering the ground quite quickly. His shoulders sloped, and his beige-coloured suit, beautifully cut, nevertheless contrived to conceal the muscular strength of his tall body.

No one approached him.

At the end of the promenade, he hailed a taxi. He sat back in it, watching through the rear window, still sure that he was not followed. They were held up for a few minutes while a horse drawing a fiacre clip-clopped along, ignoring the traffic. Horns began to blare. Palfrey kept seeing Julia Shawn's face in his mind's eye, and then the unknown woman's face. She had not even told him her name, remember — he knew absolutely nothing about her.

Was she at the ship, yet?

Or could she have been rescued, on the way to it? Had he been a fool to leave her to Duval's men? Had he been right to assume that "they" would never dream that he had sent her to the ship?

10

VIGIL

PALFREY stepped into Julia Shawn's cabin. The laundry basket was on the bed; as far as he could see, it had not been opened. The canvas straps were in position, and it was standing the right way up. He closed and locked the door behind him, then pulled the straps out of the buckles and raised the lid. Not until then was he fully satisfied; the strange woman was there. She had not stirred, and did not appear to be breathing. In a moment of alarm, Palfrey tossed the pillows on one side, drew her to a sitting position, and lifted her out.

She was breathing.

And — she was so very lovely!

He rested her on the bed, took the laundry basket away, and sat down. On the way here, while he had been on the look out for men following him, while he had been fighting back fears for this girl and for Julia, his subconscious mind must have been working hard; he had learned to trust it. Now he knew that he must do nothing to shock his captive into consciousness because it might do irreparable harm, and if that were done there would be nothing to learn from her. But sooner or later she would come out of the coma.

Need he have even a moment's doubt?

He got up, checked that the porthole was closed and secured, and went out. He closed and locked the bedroom door. The broad-faced sergeant-at-arms was on duty.

"Is the lady coming back, sir?"

Palfrey grinned.

"She's back."

"*Back?*" Scepticism made the man's voice shrill. "But I've been here all the time. All they took in was a laundry basket — *strewth!*"

"That's right," Palfrey said. "We didn't want anyone to know she was back on board — we thought she would be safer that way. So we smuggled her in. You need to take just as many precautions, though."

"Trust me," the sergeant-at-arms said. His grin seemed to split his broad face in two. "That's a smart trick, that is — fooled me all right."

The implication was that if it could fool him, it could fool anybody. The important thing was that he thought Julia was back. Soon everyone who mattered on board would think the same, so the precautions would not be relaxed. Palfrey began to consider the most effective way of making sure that "they" could not find out for certain where the girl–woman was. The *Seafarer* seemed as safe a place as any, and could be protected more easily, in some ways, than a hotel, or anywhere on land. On the other hand, "they" operated from the sea, so a ship might be more vulnerable. Moreover, there were anti-radiation shelters pitted all over the Alpes Maritimes, and any one of these was at Z5's disposal.

"But if I hide her there, I've little freedom of action," he mused. "Sooner or later I'll need her as a bait."

He would soon be able to discuss the situation with Stefan, whose detachment and good sense never failed.

One thing was certain: the girl–woman mustn't stay in Julia's cabin for long. It would be much better to have a suite, where he could keep watch part of the time, and where someone would always be at her side, to send for him the moment she showed any signs of coming round.

He went along to the Chief Purser's office. The Purser, a tall, thoughtful-looking man, had known that Simon Alting worked for one of the intelligence departments, and knew enough about Palfrey to spring to attention when he entered. He exerted himself to be helpful.

"Very glad to say that young Alting is going to pull through," he said. "He'll be convalescent for some time, I'm afraid, not much use to you, but there's no need to worry about him. . . . What can I do for you?" . . . He listened, half frowning, made heavy weather of it, and finally said: "Well, Mr and Mrs Owen and their son — I mean the *Owens* are going back home. They lost their only son, you know — swept overboard. Awful business. She's almost prostrate. He's flying her home — I *believe* they've left." He checked his passenger lists. "Yes, they have — caught a morning plane. Now if you would like that suite it's a very good one, main deck, amidships, very little movement there even in the roughest weather . . .

"Only a few doors away from Miss Shawn, too. . . . Oh, yes, I could make sure that no one's in the passage while she moves from one to the other. No trouble at all."

* * *

Palfrey carried his prisoner. She was very light, and not by any means a dead weight, although she was still in the coma and showed no sign of coming out of it.

* * *

Palfrey locked the bedroom door on her, after making sure that the portholes in it were secured — he must leave as little as possible to chance. He stepped across the drawing-room, which was almost as plush as the one at the hotel, and as he did so the telephone bell rang. He went across and picked it up. It was now nearly one o'clock, and he was feeling hungry; hunger was always a good sign, it suggested that he was coping with the situation, and was less worried than he had been.

"This is Dr Palfrey."

"Dr Palfrey," a man said in an unfamiliar voice, "you could not have committed a greater act of folly."

Palfrey said, softly: "Than what?"

"You know perfectly well what I mean. You will bring her to the yacht basin at Cannes. You will be there in two hours — at three o'clock precisely. You will bring her in a closed car, sitting behind you, and no one else will be in the car. When you have reached the basin, you will get out of the car and walk away. You will not turn back. I trust you understand."

"I — ah — I understand what you mean," Palfrey said.

There were times when he could sound and appear foolish, almost inane; and often he chose that as a kind of defence at moments when he was not quite sure what to do. "Whether I'll obey is a different matter."

"You will do what I say, or I shall send this woman agent of yours back. Dead."

"Oh," said Palfrey. "That would be a pity." There was nothing foolish or inane about his expression, although there was a vacillating note in his voice. "I shouldn't really, you know. The dead aren't any use to us. Unless of course you've really discovered the secret of re-incarnation, and everlasting life. I mean in the physical sense, not the spiritual."

The man said: "How much did she tell you of such things? She cannot have said much, or you would never have refused her what she wanted."

After a split second, Palfrey went on in the same kind of dithering voice:

"Oh, I don't know. The trouble with people like you is that you assume that you're the only ones with methods of persuasion and — but never mind. No dice. You'd be silly to kill Julia Shawn. She's much too nice a girl, and I'm sure your envoy is, too. Very charming, if a little sleepy. I thought that we might try electric shock treatment. I'm told that——"

"You must not!"

"Oh, dear," said Palfrey. "Do I detect a note of alarm? How obliging of you. Electric shock treatment wouldn't do her any good, then. Well, I'll suspend operations for a short while, if you'll do the same with Julia Shawn. Why don't we meet?"

"Palfrey, if Leah is harmed——"

"You feel about Leah as I feel about Julia, obviously," Palfrey interrupted. "I think you've had it all your own way for too long. Or thought you had. You'd be surprised if you knew how much we've been thinking about you, and why we had Corvell so closely watched. I repeat — why don't we meet?"

"I have told you what to do. Do it."

"Oh, dear," repeated Palfrey, as if forlorn. "I can't, you know. I simply can't."

Then he forced himself to ring off.

He stood close to the telephone, with a hand at his forehead; he could feel the sweat. He was covered in sweat as if he were in an oven. He swallowed the lump in his throat, then moved to the bathroom, poured ice-cold water out of the Thermos jug, and sipped it. He had hung up on the unknown man when he wanted more than anything else to talk to him. It had been delivering an ultimatum without really knowing the odds.

The water was good.

Soon, he felt cooler.

"Leah," he said to himself. "Her name is Leah. And she matters to him."

The question was — did this Leah matter enough to the man who was obviously a key figure among "they"? There was no way of telling; the answer would come if Julia Shawn were delivered to him, dead.

He told himself that it would not happen; that the man would not have spoken with such feeling unless his Leah had mattered almost beyond price, but — he must wait. Waiting was always an ordeal. He went into the bedroom and glanced at the girl–woman, said "Leah", in a husky voice, checked that the portholes were secured, and left her alone again. He ordered a steak with French fried potatoes and baked endive, with Camembert cheese to follow. Then he lit a cigarette and crossed to the porthole. He could see a great number of small boats, riding in the harbour. A white cabin cruiser sailed by, slow, majestic; two fishing boats passed. The harbour was always busy, never still.

Palfrey tried to concentrate on what the man had said, and one thing seemed significant: Palfrey sheered away from it, because it was so improbable, yet it might prove to be all important. He had said: "The dead aren't any use to us, unless of course you've really discovered the secret of re-incarnation and everlasting life." Instead of rejecting that impatiently, the man had said: "How much did she tell you of such things? She cannot have said much." He seemed to have assumed that Leah had put the idea of re-incarnation and everlasting life into Palfrey's mind, whereas he had made an obvious retort.

There was a tap at the door. Palfrey opened it cautiously, saw a waiter and the chunky-faced sergeant-at-arms outside; this was all right. He waited until the man had opened the table and put out the food, locked the door on him, then took the shiny silver coloured lid off the steak. It looked delicious. He ate too quickly, and afterwards felt sluggish and tired; he had slept very little the night before. It was absurd to tell himself that he alone must keep vigil by Leah's side, but for the time being that was how he felt. He needed more agents from London, agents who could be sent anywhere at a moment's notice, whom he could be sure would protect this girl with their lives.

First, talk to Andromovitch.

"No," Palfrey said sharply. "I'll talk to Merritt." He put in a call at once, but there was some delay. As he waited, his eyes seemed very heavy. It wasn't surprising, he told himself, but he didn't often feel as tired as this. He half dozed. Then he woke up with a jerk, and thought almost in panic: "Have I been drugged?"

Could anyone have got at his food? Was it worth trying to check?

Then he thought: This is how *she* began to lose consciousness.

He was standing in the middle of the big room, alarmed because of what might be happening to him, when the telephone bell rang. It seemed to break through the tension. He strode across and whipped the receiver off.

"Your call to London, *m'sieu*."

"Ah," Palfrey said. "Thank you." In a moment he heard Merritt's voice. "Alec — how are things with you?"

"How are things with you is more the question," Merritt said gruffly. "Sap — I've just finished a telephone conversation with a madman."

Palfrey didn't speak.

"He wouldn't give his name," Merritt went on. "He seems to think that you've kidnapped his daughter. He told me that unless I can persuade you to do what he told you to do, he'll give a demonstration of power which will terrify you." After a pause, Merritt went on: "He *was* mad, wasn't he?" The question was almost pleading.

"I hope so," Palfrey said. "I certainly hope so." He was thinking: "So he knows Z5's number. Could he have an agent with us?" "Alec, I want the latest reports on all phenomena at sea, and especially on any sight of a small fast moving craft, silver in colour — particularly any midget submarines or amphibious craft."

"Oh," said Merritt. "Then he wasn't mad."

"I think he meant whatever he said," replied Palfrey. "Now, this is even more urgent. I would like either Dr Smythe-Paterson or Dr Ephraim Higgins standing by for an emergency consultation which might have to be here in Nice, or might be anywhere between here and London. See what you can arrange, will you? I've a case of hypnotic coma, and need the best opinion I can get."

"All right, Sap. What do you think is on?"

"I don't know yet," Palfrey said. Thoughts, fears and recollections were crowding into his mind, and he went on: "Do you remember Professor Garri-Garri?"

"Garri," repeated Merritt. "Garri-*Garri*. You mean the live-for-ever Hindu who died ten years ago?"

"I mean the man who boasted that he had found the secret of extending human life indefinitely," Palfrey said. "He disappeared off the coast of Portugal, and was presumed dead."

"My *God*," breathed Merritt.

"Get all you can about him. Find out who worked with him. Find out whether any of his assistants have developed ideas of their own. Put our best men onto this. Call New York and ask them to get busy on the same inquiry." Now that the idea was sprouting in his mind, Palfrey could not give instructions quickly enough. "I can't be sure that I'm on the right lines but if I am the quicker we know all there is to know, the better. Now——"

He broke off.

The first he knew of the horror that was about to descend upon that harbour was a screaming voice and the thudding of footsteps on the passage outside. Next moment, the ship's hooter roared the six short, six long blasts which told of fierce alarm. Almost at once, whistles shrilled out.

"What's happening there?" Merritt called urgently. "I can hear——"

"Listen," Palfrey said. "If anything goes wrong, try to stop this girl Leah from being taken away. If there's a ghost of a chance of——"

A great *eeeeeehhhhh* of sound smashed across his words. As it came he felt a tremendous jolt. The ship was hurled against the quayside. He felt it shudder, heard the crashing of heavy weights, heard a crunching sound. He was flung off his feet. He did not try to save himself but turned his back to the wall, and took the worst of the impact on his buttocks. He fell down. The door swung open, both hinges smashed. The bedroom door banged. The whole ship seemed to be shuddering, and the noise was of thunder echoing and echoing about the passages, on deck, on the stricken harbour beyond.

11
ACT OF TERROR

VERY slowly, Palfrey picked himself up. There was sharp pain in his right leg from the thigh downwards, and his whole body seemed bruised and tender. He stretched out a hand to touch a chair, staggered, and quickly took his weight off that bruised leg. The room was in chaos. Chairs upturned, pictures on the floor, drawers out and contents strewn all over the floor, cushions off the chairs in an untidy heap; oddments from the writing table were at his feet.

He could hear shouting, the crash of falling debris; and screaming.

He tried to walk again, testing his leg gingerly, found that he could put a little weight on it, and limped towards the bedroom door. He was almost frightened of what he might find, but need not have been. The head of the bed had been jammed against the wall by the dressing table, and had not shifted much. The girl–woman lay on it. She was further over on one side than the other, the bedclothes had been shaken off as if a giant hand had snatched at them. Her slender legs, bare from the thighs, were on one side, the feet over the edge of the bed; but she was still unconscious.

A man came running.

"Are you all right, sir? Are you——"

Palfrey turned to the outer door, and his leg gave way. He pitched forward almost into the arms of the chunky sergeant-at-arms, whose face was bleeding from a cut on the forehead, and whose uniform was rumpled and covered in dust.

"Sir!"

Palfrey picked himself up.

"Nothing much," he said. "What's the damage?"

"God *knows*, sir!"

"Like that, is it?"

"Blimey, it shoved me a hundred feet down the passage, and every door's open. Looks like a bloody battlefield. What's happening, Dr Palfrey?"

Palfrey said bleakly: "That was a simple, ruthless act of terror." He was thinking how often such a thing as this had happened in the past, when one man or a group of men had believed that they could impose their will upon the world. Once thwarted, even if seriously challenged, all they could usually do was to attack with this kind of blind savagery.

"There must be *hundreds* dead." The sergeant-at-arms gulped. "God knows how many have been swept out to sea, that must have hit the beach good and proper."

Palfrey half-closed his eyes.

The hateful, hurtful noise was greater; people were moaning, more were shouting, one woman was screaming. Horns were blowing, whistles shrilling, and men and women were moving about the ship. He stepped into the passage. Right and left he could see the mess — two girls were on their backs, one of them bleeding from a cut on the leg, another from the nose. Stewards were making their way about, shakily. He saw a nurse with blood splashed all over her uniform.

"You go and see what you can do to help," Palfrey said.

"My orders are to stay with you, sir."

Palfrey said: "Yes, of course. All right." He limped back into the room. His leg felt easier, and he could walk with reasonable comfort, although he probably wouldn't be able to run for a long time. He stood looking at Leah. He kept hearing that voice in his head, feeling quite sure that if he had agreed to do what the man had said, this would not have happened. He, Palfrey, was responsible for what had come about; or rather, he could have stopped it.

The beach crowds, the happy children, the sun-bathers, the sea-bathers, the young and the old — oh, God. It was anguish.

Footsteps sounded, and he turned to see the Captain, big, bluff, burly, very pale.

"Are you all right, Palfrey?"

"Yes. Thanks."

"What's happening?"

Palfrey said simply: "We're being blackmailed."

"*Black*mailed?"

"Yes."

"Listen," the Captain interrupted, "I've just had a message from a reliable source. I'm told that this happened because you are keeping a girl here against her will. I said that it was nonsense, but I would check. Miss Shawn's not being kept against her will, is she?"

"No," said Palfrey. "Not Miss Shawn. What was this reliable source?"

"A highly-placed Customs official in Nice."

"What is his name?"

"What the devil does that matter?" demanded the Captain. He pushed past Palfrey to the door of the bedroom, and stared at the girl–woman on the bed. "*That's* not Miss Shawn." There was a note of accusation in his voice.

"No."

"Palfrey, are you keeping——"

"I wonder if you'll do something for me," Palfrey said. "Send a message by radio telephone to your main office in London. Ask them to check with the Admiralty. I think you'll find that they will instruct you to do whatever I——" he hesitated, almost said "say", but substituted "ask". "There have been earlier attempts at blackmail, you know. Hitler, for instance."

"I know all about Hitler," the Captain said roughly. "But thousands have been killed. Don't you understand? The beaches are absolute shambles. Thousands——"

"Keep your head!" Palfrey said, sharply. "We're not children."

The Captain looked as if he would explode, somehow kept silent, glared at Palfrey, turned on his heel and said over his shoulder:

"The Admiralty had better back you up."

He went out.

Palfrey was not worried about the Admiralty. He was wondering how to get this girl–woman away from here. He had been wrong before. The ship was too vulnerable. True, the attack might never have been launched had the Patriarch known Leah was on board, but that wasn't the point; the point was that he had to keep her alive. The safest place was one of the radiation shelters, but the difficulty now was to get her to one. Duval was his main hope. The telephone lines would be down, though, and it would not be easy to get in touch with the local chief of Z5. He was not likely to be allowed to take the girl–woman out of the cabin, certainly not off the ship, until the Captain had received his confirmation from the Admiralty.

He could start getting her ready.

If he had to carry her out again, if anyone had to carry her out——

It would be easy! There must be dozens of injured people on board, ambulances would be outside — or vans or private cars, anything which could be converted into ambulances. He hated the picture of the scene, but in the confusion there should surely be no difficulty in getting the girl out of this place, and to one where not even a freak wave could hurt her.

But it could hurt plenty of others.

He turned back into the bedroom, and began to dress the girl. Her body was limp, but the flesh was firm and warm — this was sleep which seemed quite natural. In the midst of all the chaos, the woman Leah was at peace.

*   *   *

The Captain came back.

"I am to give you all the help I can," he said, almost humbly. "If I lost my temper, I'm sorry."

"Who wouldn't?" asked Palfrey. "Thanks. I need a car or preferably a van——"

"There is a man named Duval waiting along the passage," said the Captain. "He tells me that he has a car at your disposal. Seems worried about you, too. Will you see him?"

"I can't see him soon enough," Palfrey said.

Duval, whom he knew fairly well, was a short, rather plump man, very French even to a pointed beard, but otherwise smooth-shaven, looking rather as if he had just been powdered and pomaded. The plump hand was very firm when he gripped. He searched Palfrey's face, as if looking for signs of injury, and said:

"I am glad you are no worse. I think perhaps you need to move the woman."

"I do," said Palfrey.

"Against such emergency I have arranged for one of the radiation shelters to be made ready," Duval said. "It is beyond Grasse. I have the car outside, and if you wish we can start at once. I warn you that it will be difficult at first, there is so much — damage, so much injury. But we shall get through. I have arranged for the police to clear a way for us, and once we are at the back of the town it will not be so difficult. We must go along the Promenade des Anglais for some distance, however — a number of lorries crashed into each other when the wave struck the sea wall. They burst into flames. So we cannot drive to the back of the town from here."

Palfrey said: "Let's go whichever way we can."

Between them, they carried Leah. Many men were carrying or helping to carry women and girls. Some were being carried on improvised stretchers, some on chairs. Many were limping. As he walked off the ship Palfrey saw *thousands* of injured people, saw the wreckage of hundreds of small boats floating on a sea which was now peaceful. Soon, they were out in the open, away from the docks. Everywhere it sounded as if a great lament was rising from the throats of the people. On the landward side of the great promenade, the hotels were hardly damaged, but instead of people sitting at their leisure with the orchestras playing, emergency dressing stations littered every terrace. More and more injured were being taken into the hotels. On the other side, all the chairs were on the road; some must have been dragged back into the sea when the wave had subsided. On the wet sidewalks, dotted with puddles, were the wooden rests on which people sun-bathed, the gay umbrellas, the tiny wooden dressing *cabinettes*, the wreckage of small boats — and people.

It was one of the most awful sights Palfrey had ever seen.

There were *people*, floating, face downwards; dead by drowning. There were many hundreds. Their stillness as they lay on the still water was in strange, awful contrast to the movement of swimmers, of men in pedalos, men searching for their lost ones, for any who were not dead. All along the beach, hundreds of people close to the water's edge were bending over hundreds of others. They were giving artificial respiration, all in various stages of hope and of despair.

Duval said: "It is the worst day we have ever known here, Dr Palfrey."

"I can believe it," Palfrey said. "Do you know the chief Customs officer?"

"He talked to me after he had talked to the Captain of the *Seafarer*," Duval interrupted. "He told me that he had received a telephone message just before the wave came. He said that a man had told him that what was about to happen was because you had kidnapped a woman, and would not release her. He did not know whether to believe it or not, but when the wave actually came——" Duval broke off. "I *saw* it."

Palfrey caught his breath.

"There was a flash," went on Duval, in an awed voice. "It seemed to ride along the sea, which was so calm after the early morning wind. Then for a mile in each direction a great wall of water rose. It was like a series of bombs going off beneath the sea. A long wave rose up out of a perfectly calm sea. I *saw* it, Dr Palfrey. What kind of man can do this thing? — what kind of man would be prepared to do it?"

Palfrey said: "That is what we're going to find out."

"And this is the woman he wants?"

"Yes," Palfrey said.

"I have tried to make sure that we cannot be followed," said Duval, after a pause. "I have given instructions that any car or anything on wheels which comes after us be delayed for at least fifteen minutes. We can only hope that the effort succeeds. But——" he paused again, looked sideways at Palfrey, and then asked in a hushed voice: "If it does, if we take this woman to a place where this man cannot find her — what will he do, Palfrey? Where next will the horror strike?"

12

LIMBO

PALFREY did not attempt to answer the question. Duval seemed to expect no answer. Soon, they passed out of the area of destruction, but at once ran into another complication. Traffic which had been coming along the coast road from Cannes and from the airport was held up in one enormous block. Crowds of people were moving along the promenades, thronging towards the scene of disaster. Small ships and large were heading for the scene, too, and the sea was a mass of small craft. A few ambulances and fire engines, summoned from Cannes to help with the chaos, were jammed in with the traffic.

At last Palfrey and Duval turned off.

Palfrey looked round, and saw Leah, stretched out on the back seat; sleeping.

It was nearly an hour before they passed through Grasse. In the perfume city excitement was at fever pitch, but on the lonely mountain roads everything was calm. Near the valley where the shelter was built, Duval's men and some military personnel had been warned, and preparation had been made for the new arrivals. There was no delay once Duval established their identity. They were escorted into a huge man-made cave, lit dimly by electricity generated from a plant inside the mountains, and then into a big steel lift. Once they were inside this, steel doors closed about them, and they began to move down slowly; twice, Palfrey saw that great doors closed above them, they were being sealed off at several points, so that there was no risk at all of radiation. Soon, they reached the bottom of the shelter. They stepped out into a wide passage, in a big, bare place which was unusual only because there were no windows. A few soldiers stood about, on duty.

A young officer, leading them, stopped at some double doors, and pressed a button on one side. The doors slid open.

"This is the apartment reserved for you," he announced.

Except that it was furnished sparsely, it might have been a hotel suite.

"Just before I left I was told by Merritt that Dr Ephraim Higgins will come to see the patient," Duval said. "I will bring him here. Will you wait for him, Dr Palfrey?"

"No," Palfrey said. "I'd better be back in Nice or London, but readily available. I hope this woman's leader will want to talk to me again."

Duval said nothing.

Palfrey took a last look at Leah, who had been exactly as she was now for several hours. Then he went back the way he had come, as sure as he could be that the woman could not be taken away without authority.

Who else was safe?

At the surface, the sun was high and very warm. As Palfrey and Duval drove back towards the coast, they had a glimpse of a calm, sunlit ocean, dotted here and there with small boats. Two liners, untouched by freak wave or heavy seas, seemed to steam like toy ships on painted water.

"Where will you go now?" Duval asked.

"Back to the hotel," Palfrey said. "And I'll wait."

Waiting was going to be the worst thing of all, because as he waited he would think of so much — of Corvell, of the disaster here, of the fact that "they" must have been active for two years at least and he had had no knowledge of it. He would think of the men who had disappeared as well as of those thousands who had died — and would keep brooding over Julia Shawn, wondering what had happened to her, and how the man he knew as the Patriarch might use her in order to get what he wanted.

In Palfrey's room was a sealed package from London. He opened it by a window, and the breeze fluttered some of the papers inside. These were reports, typewritten on flimsy paper, from a dozen Z5 agents. Some dealt with the phenomena at sea, and Palfrey felt a sense of increasing excitement as well as fear when he confirmed that most of the disappearances at sea had been preceded by freak waves. No other report of a midget silver-coloured vessel or submarine was here.

But there were reports of the Indian, Garri-Garri, together with two photographs of the man. The reports confirmed Palfrey's own recollection. Garri-Garri had been a Hindu scientist who had spent his life studying the problem of longevity and the evidence for reincarnation. He had claimed, at times, that he had turned men and women in their seventies into vigorous people of young middle-age. One or two instances had been investigated, with inconclusive results. Garri-Garri had never been proved a charlatan but few scientists or doctors of repute had been greatly impressed by him. Every report revealed him as a man of overwhelming pride, arrogance and vanity. He had stormed out of several conferences when his integrity had been challenged — always in the same way. The accusation was that the young and vigorous people had *not* been the older ones rejuvenated, but different people. Garri-Garri had sworn that this was calumny.

Had he lied?

He had disappeared off the coast near Cascais, Portugal, when deep sea fishing, but there was nothing to indicate that this had followed a freak wave.

Palfrey read all these reports, then turned again to the photographs of the handsome man with dark, dominating eyes.

The girl–woman prisoner was so like him that she might indeed be his daughter.

*   *   *

Julia Shawn did not know where she was.

She was alive, she was fully conscious, she was frightened — partly because of being alone in a small room. The one thing about the room which puzzled her most *was* its smallness. It was not much larger than a tiny cabin on a cross-channel steamer. She was on the lower bunk. The other was a foot or two above her, and by stretching out her arms she could just touch the far wall. She turned over, and saw that her clothes were folded over a chair. Then she thought:

"They can't be *my* clothes."

She sat up, almost bumped her head, moved more cautiously and touched the clothes. No, they weren't hers. The dress was yellow, by coincidence presumably, but the sandals were brown, like pliable leather — or were they of plastic? There were no stockings, but there was an almost transparent brassiere and a pair of flimsy panties.

She pushed the single sheet back. The first thing she noticed was its feather-lightness; it was like gossamer. The substance puzzled her. It was obviously strong, but lighter in weight than any material she knew.

She got off the bed, having to keep her head low because of the bunk above. There was only just room between that bunk and the ceiling for someone to get onto it. It was empty. A gossamer sheet, like the one on her bunk, was spread smoothly over it. She made herself look away from it, and then picked up the brassiere; it was made of the same kind of material, and it seemed absurd to imagine that it would give her any support. She put it on, bending down to fit it over her full breasts; when she straightened up, she felt the support to be both firm and substantial. She pulled on the fragile pair of panties, and had never touched fabric so delicate; yet when she pulled, it seemed very tough.

She put on the "dress".

In fact, the garment was more like a gym tunic. It was slightly waisted, and the pleated skirt fell halfway between her waist and her knees. It would make an ideal dress for tennis, except for the colour. It was also so light in weight that she hardly felt as if she had anything on.

She stood as far back as she could, in front of a small wall mirror, but could only see her head and shoulders.

Suddenly, she raised her hands; quite startled.

She was surprisingly calm, and only a little frightened. She had come round from the drug, realised that she was a prisoner, and yet her only reaction had been of curiosity. Until this moment, she had felt no fear. Now that she had reminded herself of reason for fear, it swept over her like a wave. She stared at the door in a kind of terror which made her whole body quiver.

Nothing happened.

She clenched her teeth as she reached out and touched the handle of the door. It would be locked, of course. She turned the handle and pulled — and the door opened.

She stood quite still; holding her breath.

The small door was rather like a hatch, and she could not get out without bending her head. She made herself go forward. Her hips touched the sides of the door, and although she bent very low, the top of her head bumped. But next moment she was in a narrow passage, where the ceiling was little more than head high.

It was like being in a miniature prison; a kind of dolls' house of a prison.

She heard no sound.

Her heart was palpitating, but she made herself go on. She kept thinking of what Palfrey had said: it did not matter what she saw or felt or touched — any trifling thing might help to identify this place later. But — the walls were bare. They were a pale green in colour, not unpleasing in itself, but there was no relief from it; no darker line, no change of colour, no break — even the outlines of doors were barely discernible. She walked on, towards a T-junction. The passage there stretched out a long way in each direction. She saw only two things in the passage, one on either side; each reminded her of a steel door, like those on ships to divide one section from another.

Which way should she go?

Why had she *any* freedom of movement?

She turned right, and walked along, heart in mouth. She thought for a while that the walls at either end were blank, that she was surrounded by three passages, and that was all; but when she reached the end she saw another passage, leading in either direction.

Again she turned right.

Then a long way ahead, she saw what looked like a big

shadow on the wall, the only relief she had seen yet from the pale green. She glanced upwards. At intervals there were little grilles rather like those of a miniature radio set. The air was fresh, and yet it wasn't like the atmosphere of a house which was often open to the fresh air. The light was uniform; that helped to explain the uniformity of the colour, too.

What was the shadow?

As she drew nearer, she saw that it was more like a big window. It must be at least twenty feet long by six feet high, and it looked very dark outside. Was it night? She drew closer to the window, and saw a faint sheen, as of glass. She held her breath, scared for some reason she could not understand. It was not just that she seemed to be alone, that there had been no sound anywhere, and that she had no idea where she was. There was disquieting eeriness, particularly about that "window".

Was it one?

She reached it — and almost cried out.

She was looking out into water; deep water. She saw a huge fish heading straight for the window, and shrank back. It stayed some distance away, unblinking, then turned and swam lazily off. A small octopus had eyes in its hooded body-cum-head like a Peeping Tom from a new planet; its tentacles waved sluggishly. A cloud of fish, all small, all with faintly pink bellies, flashed past her and disappeared. A school of tropical fish, strangely shaped and beautifully coloured, passed like a regiment of toy soldiers. She saw more big fish, including one that she believed was a shark.

All the time, the water in which they swam seemed motionless; the fish created the only movement.

Julia moistened her lips, and realised how very dry they were. Her mouth was parched, too. She looked away, but found herself forced to glance back; the eyes of a big fish seemed so close to hers. She shuddered, and swung round — and *screamed*.

A man stood just behind her.

She backed away, tripped, and nearly fell. The man

stretched out a hand, took her wrist, and held her until she was steady. Then he let her go. She saw that he was smiling faintly — not grinning at her, as she had thought at first; he looked as if he were mildly amused, that was all. He was about five feet six in height, very little taller than she. He wore a blue smock, rather like the one she was wearing, but it was shorter. It reminded her of the dress which Roman soldiers had worn, but this man wore nothing on his head. His fair hair was trimmed in a kind of crew cut. His broad features were pleasant, not particularly handsome but quite attractive. His skin was flawless.

It reminded Julia of the girl's skin; the girl who had started all this.

"Hallo," the man said, in perfectly good English. "I am sorry if I frightened you."

She realised she was gasping for breath.

"I — I'm all right."

"Of course you are," he said. "This is the safest place in the world — or one of them." His smile showed that he had good, even teeth. "How long have you been here?"

"Not — not long."

"How are you feeling?"

"I — I tell you I'm all right," she insisted.

"I'm not at all sure that you are." He stretched out his hand and took her wrist; he was feeling her pulse. "Not bad," he conceded. "Better than I expected. Are you hungry?"

"No."

"I think you ought to have something, anyhow," he said. "Come along with me, and we'll have a light meal. You can have very little food, if you prefer." He took her arm, turned round, and led her back the way she had come. She was still frightened and nervous, but could not deny that this man seemed to give her a kind of reassurance. He was probably in the middle twenties, she guessed. His arms and legs were well shaped, and the skin smooth and — *without blemish*, she reminded herself.

He stopped beneath one of the small grilles in the roof, and raised his right hand. That was all — he raised his right hand. Immediately, a door in the wall began to open. It slid to the right. Beyond, she saw light and colour — *and people*. The man stood aside. Julia had to step over a ledge, and bend low to get through, but there was reasonable room. The door slid to behind them.

Now it seemed as if she was in a huge office with glass walls. Men and women were at desks, much as they would be in any office. On a wall — that on the right and beyond the offices — was a mass of instruments, and it reminded her of an atomic research station where she had once worked on security. No one appeared to take any notice of her. As they neared a door at the far end of this central passage, she realised that all the people were dressed alike — the women as she was, and the men like her companion.

It was then, as they stepped through another doorway, that the truth hit her with almost physical violence. The explanation of that huge window and the big fish came to her belatedly but with overwhelming effect.

They were under water; at the bottom of the sea.

13

THE DEEP

FOR a moment, Julia stood quite still; shocked, frightened. The young man put his hand up, as he had outside, and a door slid open in front of him. Only when he stood inside, for her to pass, did he notice that she hadn't followed close behind him. He turned round.

He must have seen how shocked she was, but he smiled and stretched out his hand.

"Come with me, I will look after you," he said, as if he were talking to a child.

She took his hand, and he led her out of this passage, into

another. For the first time, colour appeared on the walls —
waves of different hues which had a subtle effect, as if — like
a rainbow — they touched the air with their diversity, as one
merged into the next. The colour on walls and ceiling was
faintly iridescent, as if it was shining through water.

Julia did not think of that consciously. The man's grip was
firm on her arm, and she went forward in a daze. She did
notice that instead of the bare offices and desks on either side,
there were armchairs and couches. Men and women sat about,
some reading books, others reading newspapers. At the end of
one room was a smaller place, partitioned off. In one wall of
this was a television screen, and for the first time, Julia really
took notice; for the people on the screen were dressed in
ordinary clothes. Suddenly, a large face appeared, and she
recognised the character of Perry Mason. That brought a
moment of realism, almost of relief.

Before her guide raised his hand in front of the next door,
it slid open. A girl on the other side said:

"Hallo, Boris."

"Maria," the young man said, "this is Julia Shawn, who
has come on a visit."

"From above?" the girl asked. She looked Julia up and
down with a curiosity and interest which was almost childlike
in its frankness.

"Yes."

"I often wonder how it is up there these days," Maria said.
"Is it still chaotic? Are human beings still imbecilic in their
attitudes towards one another?"

"I hope that the Patriarch will arrange a general discussion
before Julia goes back," Boris said. "I will inform you."

"Oh." Maria was momentarily taken aback; she gave the
impression that she was suddenly apprehensive. "Yes, of
course. I'm sorry."

She pushed past.

Julia found herself wanting to ask: "Why should she be
sorry?" Was she frightened even of the mention of the
Patriarch?

Boris led her through this doorway into another room — a restaurant. Here the colours were subtly different, and the contrasts greater. Small tables stood about, with comfortable looking chairs around them. Several small groups sat at the tables, eating and drinking. Almost at once Julia noticed that men as well as girls moved about, serving the food — and that they were dressed almost exactly as those whom they were serving. A few glanced across at the newcomers, but no one moved towards them. Boris went to a table in a corner, and pulled out a chair.

"Please sit down," he said.

She sat down.

"May I order for you?"

"I'm not really hungry."

"We'll see," said Boris. He pressed the table, and spoke as if to someone who wasn't here. "Delicacy, please." He removed his fingers, and Julia saw that he had pressed a kind of push-button which was raised a fraction of an inch above the level of the table. She saw more; at first sight the table — like the walls here — had seemed to be a simple pattern of colour, but gradually positive shapes appeared. She could make out the silhouettes of mountain ranges, but none which was familiar. In her bewildered, half-frightened, half-curious mood, this puzzled her, but she did not comment.

"Would you like to ask questions?" Boris inquired.

Julia didn't reply.

"You are free to do so, and I am free to answer," he said. "The Patriarch has given me permission."

After a pause, Julia found herself asking: "Who *is* the Patriarch?"

"Our leader."

"Whose leader?"

"The Deep's," he said.

The answer came easily, as if there was nothing strange about it. "*The Deep's.*" She recalled the great glass window and the monsters as well as the tiny creatures of the oceans which she had seen, and she felt again the sense of shock which had seemed to explode within her when she had realised that she was in some great under-water place.

Place?

This was huge — a vast building, covering many acres. She must have seen at least five hundred people here already. How many more were there? How much more was there to see?

"I don't understand you," she said.

Boris smiled in that charming way of his, and she had the impression that her answer gave him a great deal of satisfaction.

"You really don't understand, do you?"

"No."

"Yet you would, if Palfrey knew."

She answered a little too quickly: "Palfrey keeps a great deal to himself."

"Not as much as that," he said. "All our reports are the same — that no one up above even suspects the existence of The Deep."

She did not really know what it was, and she felt sure that Palfrey had no idea. He had sent her here to find out every-thing that she could, and had told her that a single glimpse, a word, a tone of voice, could help him — help the world — to find out what was happening. The more she learned, the more effectively she would be doing her job. At the back of her mind lurked the fear that she might never see Palfrey again, might never be able to tell him what she knew, but that fear stayed in the background.

And Palfrey had said: "Don't do anything which makes the danger greater. Play along with them if you get half a chance." His voice almost seemed to echo about this room.

A girl brought a tray on which were two covered dishes, much as they might be "up above". She smiled, as she took off one lid, and placed the dish in front of Julia. A delicate aroma arose from what looked like a thin steak. The colour was different from a steak at home; much more red. There was a pale-coloured sauce, something which looked like chipped potatoes — not big and solid, but quite small.

Boris said: "Try it."

He had the same dish in front of him.

"You will like it," the waitress assured her. "It is a deep water fish, so delicate and superbly flavoured."

The aroma seemed to be stealing into Julia's nostrils. Quite suddenly she felt ravenous. She cut off a small piece of the "steak" and put it into her mouth. The flavour was exquisite.

"Good?" asked Boris.

"Wonderful!"

"I thought you would think so. We have the best chefs known to man here, and all the secrets of the gourmets from all over the world."

"I can believe it," Julia said.

"In fact," Boris went on, "we have the best of everything."

"Have you?"

"The absolute best."

"I see," said Julia.

"You don't believe me."

"No."

"You will learn to."

"I am open to conviction," Julia assured him.

"Yes, I believe you are."

Boris went on eating and did not speak for some time. Julia found each mouthful so delicious that all she wanted to do, for the time being, was to savour the food.

Was it *all* like this?

What did Boris mean by saying that they had the "best of everything"? He sounded as if he believed it.

"Julia," he said, when she had finished, "I want you to answer me some questions. Upon your answers may depend not only your own future but the future of a great many other people, including Dr Palfrey. Please do not lie, or be evasive. We have perfected ways of compelling reluctant witnesses to talk, and — *nothing* is allowed to prevent that. Do you understand?"

"*Play along with them*," Palfrey had urged.

"I understand," she said.

"It is absolutely essential that you should answer. Some of the answers we already know, and if you lie——"

"I may have to refuse to answer," Julia interrupted. "I will not lie nor be evasive."

The little smile played about his lips.

Before he spoke again, the waitress brought a pot of coffee; or what looked like coffee. Boris poured out. Julia tasted it — and had exactly the same experience as before: it was like nectar. Coffee was the base, but it was made in a way she had never tasted before, and the aroma was enticing — as the food's had been.

"Good?" Boris was naïvely eager that she should be impressed.

"Wonderful," she said again.

"You see?" He laughed. "Now — the questions." He plunged straight into them. "Did Palfrey know anything about The Deep before today?"

"I don't think so."

"Can't you be sure?"

"Not absolutely. He keeps so much to himself."

"Has he ever said anything to suggest that he knows?"

"No."

"Why did he take such great care with Professor Corvell?"

"Because the Professor is one of the best British physicists."

"*British?*"

"Yes."

"Julia," Boris said very softly, "I warned you. I shall not warn you again."

He frightened her, not only by what he said, but how he said it. Even the tone of his voice changed, and seemed to take on menace; yet it was not simply menace. He conveyed to her a sense of the absolute inevitability of punishment by physical pain, and frightened her the more because she did not know what she had said to cause it.

"Do you understand what I mean?"

"I — I don't understand at all."

"You lied."

"I did not."

"You said that Corvell was protected — so far as protection is possible — because he was the best British physicist."

"And he is."

"Does Palfrey *really* think in such narrow national terms?"

At once, understanding dawned on her. Palfrey was international in his activities. Z5 was an international organisation. She herself had never been able completely to free herself from national values.

"Palfrey would have taken the same precautions had the professor been American or Russian," Julia answered. "Or of any nationality that subscribes to Z5."

"That is better."

"Is it part of your job to trick me into lying?"

"To trick . . ." he began, as if genuinely puzzled. Then for the first time he frowned. It was quite different from the way he had looked when he had accused her of lying — it was as if he were suddenly confronted with a difficult problem. "*Trick?*" he repeated, and then his voice rose. "You mean *deceive?*"

"I mean deceive."

"Julia," said Boris with great deliberation, "when we are up above it is sometimes necessary to use the methods of diplomacy and chicanery; to deal in half-truths and to foster misconceptions. That is never necessary in any part of The Deep. Have no doubt about that."

It did not occur to her that this was not true; she accepted it completely.

"I see," she said, almost humbly.

"Why did Palfrey concern himself so much about Corvell?" asked Boris.

"Because he has been worried by the disappearances of other men like him, or men as important to civilisation."

"*Worried?*"

"Yes."

"Did he tell you which men?"

"No."

"Did he give you any indication of their identity?"

"No," Julia answered with great deliberation.

"Did he *expect* trouble at sea?"

"He did not say so."

"Why were you and Simon Alting sent to watch over him?"

"He had been ill, and was advised to have a cruise. Wherever the professor went he had to be protected."

"Only that?"

"Yes."

"Julia," Boris asked next, in a different tone of voice which suggested increasing tension, "how much did *you* see? How much were you able to tell Palfrey?"

On that instant, Julia sensed that of all the questions, this was the most important, the one he was desperately anxious for her to answer. What she had to decide, quickly, was whether she dare lie to him; whether she had any hope of getting away with deception.

14

THE PATRIARCH

WHAT would Palfrey tell her to do? Julia asked herself desperately.

If she lied, and this man realised it, what would follow? How seriously need she take his threats? Even as the question posed itself, she knew the answer, for she recalled his expression, the way he had looked at her with a menace which had frightened. The same look appeared in his eyes, now — not so pronounced and therefore not so frightening, but unmistakable.

"Play along when you can," Palfrey had said.

"Julia," Boris said softly, "must I repeat the question?"

When he lowered his voice like that, it was as if he were shouting — as if this were his way of *raising* his voice.

"I shouldn't tell you," she said at last.

"I don't understand you."

"Don't you understand loyalty?"

"There is only one loyalty — to the Patriarch."

"I have a different one," Julia said.

Inwardly, she began to tremble.

After a long pause, when the trembling became almost uncontrollable, and she felt her fingers begin to shake, Boris said: "Wait, please."

He got up, bowed slightly from the waist, and walked off.

It was strange to sit here, alone — so utterly alone because the others in the restaurant appeared to be oblivious of her. No one even glanced her way. The waitress moved to newcomers at other tables, but did not approach her. Trying to take her mind off the immediate fears, she looked more closely at the walls. The drawing as well as the painting was of such subtle technique that the pictures seemed as if they were changing all the time. Now and again, as she turned her head to see a different wall, she had an illusion of movement; it was like looking at the walls through deep water.

That reminded her of the big window; the sharks; the Peeping Tom octopus.

In turn that reminded her of Boris and the cold menace in his expression. She began to tremble and could not stop herself. Her right arm began to shake as far as the elbow. Why had he left her so abruptly? Where had he gone? He had told her what to expect if she lied. Did he consider her refusal to tell him what she had told Palfrey a lie?

She must get rid of the shakes.

She forced herself to concentrate on the murals again. In a way they reminded her of a map of the world. But it was the kind of outline, not the shape, which did that.

Then she saw a place which looked like the British Isles in reverse. She stared at it. At last she rose slowly to her feet and went closer. No one attempted to stop her, no one appeared to notice her.

Now she had recognised one thing, other shapes fell into perspective. The Brittany Coast, the Cherbourg Peninsula —

yes, there was the north of Europe, and the Russian coastline. She had no doubt about this, now, but was still conscious of a difference she could not name.

The familiar places were flat, painted in a kind of browny-grey, although the subtle changes of shades and colouring were continually strengthening the illusion that she was looking through deep water. She thrust that thought aside. What was the difference?

Suddenly, another fact fell into place.

The British Isles, the coastline of Europe and Europe itself, were all flat. She turned to look at other walls, and realised that the land masses were *all* flat, whereas the oceans of the world were in contours, and like a skilfully drawn relief map.

It was like looking at a projection of the world in reverse, with the continents shown as seas, and the oceans shown as land masses, with ranges of mountains, deep valleys, desert stretches.

Slowly, frighteningly, the truth dawned on her. This was a huge projection of the ocean and sea beds of the world, showing the mountain ranges beneath the waters.

She stared about her, fearful in case her stupefaction should be noticed, and went slowly back to her table. She felt like shouting, screaming, doing anything to make the others take notice of her. She felt that she hated them, they were so cold, aloof, alien. She sat down. Her arm was no longer quivering — this new realisation had stilled it by making her mind work, of course, taking her mind off personal fears.

This place was under the water; everything here seemed to tone in with the sea.

Ah!

That was another thing; the different shades and colours were like the changing, differing colours of the sea.

When it was bright or with sunshine it was a pale blue.

Blue: the colour of some of the women's dresses.

When it was stormy and cloudy, it became dark and grey — like the shades of the colouring of the walls of the passages. Everything here was a reflection of or an aspect of the sea.

The *Deep*.

She found herself clenching her hands.

Then Boris came in, approached her table, and held out his right hand.

"Come, please," he said.

She could not move, she was so frightened.

"Come!" he ordered.

Her legs nearly doubled under her when she did get to her feet. Boris's grip was firm, but not tight, but after the first movement she did not want to look into his eyes for fear of what she would see. He led the way through the doorway from which they had come earlier, but instead of going past the rooms with books and the television set, they turned along a narrow passage which she had not noticed before. At a doorway, he raised his hand, and the door slid open. There was nothing miraculous about it in these days of electronics but there was something uncanny, perhaps because of the casualness with which he did it.

Julia stepped through.

Instead of an empty passage, there were two men. They were dressed exactly as the other men down here, and were about the same height. They stood opposite each other; staring. As Boris approached, one of them said:

"He is waiting."

"We are ready," Boris said.

He? Who was he? Imagination tore at Julia's mind. That moment she saw "him" as a man to be terrified of; a kind of Grand Inquisitor, ready with all manner of torture to make her talk. Boris was so close to her that it was almost as if he expected her to turn and run away.

A door opened.

It was the same kind as the others, perhaps a little larger and wider. Certainly the passage beyond was wider. There was a greater variety of colours here, and the walls were painted in an under-water scene. Myriads of tiny tropical fish seemed to move about, as if they really were swimming. The brilliant hues seemed to shimmer and scintillate as if they were precious stones, not simply the jewels of the sea.

Then Julia saw a recess on the right hand side. Sitting at a desk behind it was a man. The first thing she noticed about him was his age; he was probably in the middle fifties. His close cut hair was iron grey. He wore a grey beard, too, trimmed very close. She was vaguely reminded of Ernest Hemingway in his later years.

It was when he looked up at her that Julia realised that all the other people she had seen here were about the same age, in the middle twenties. By comparison, this man seemed old.

Before she had time to think about that, he stood up.

"Patriarch," Boris said. "This is Julia."

There was nothing ludicrous or pompous about the use of the word "Patriarch". It was uttered as naturally as if a man were saying "Father", or "Master". There was respect, even veneration in it, and absolute acceptance of this man's right to allegiance.

The Patriarch looked at her for a long time. His eyes, green as the sea, had an almost hypnotic effect; it was as if he was willing her to the same allegiance as Boris.

"So this is Julia," the older man said at last. He had a deeper voice than Boris, and there was an ironic twist to his lips. "I understand that you have divided loyalties."

"I don't think so," Julia said. Her voice was weak, her heart was thumping. "Different, but — but not divided."

"I think they are."

Julia did not respond.

She felt weak from fear and tensions, frightened of the man in front of her, and of the circumstances. The world she knew seemed so remote and far away. This was so different, so unreal — and yet there was nothing unreal about Boris and the man he called the Patriarch. Boris was no longer touching her, but she could almost feel the grip of his fingers.

"You have a loyalty to yourself, and a loyalty to Palfrey and all he stands for," the Patriarch said. "They now come into conflict."

"I see them as one," she made herself say.

"Whatever the cost?" There was a hint of menace in the

way he said that, creating a fear of unnameable horrors. She
had to steel herself to answer:

"Yes."

After a pause the Patriarch spoke more briskly. She had the
feeling that he had finished the preliminaries, and had made
up his mind what to do. As she stared back at him, the image
of Palfrey seemed to hover at his shoulders; Palfrey, pondering,
twisting those strands of hair at his forehead, so human.

Human.

These people lacked a quality which Palfrey had in such
abundance: the warmth of humanity.

"It is as well to be frank," the Patriarch said. "I can make
you talk, of course. I dislike using such pressure, but do not
shrink from it. Now, answer my questions as I put them,
please."

Julia said: "I will try."

"Did you see anything when you stood on the deck of the
Seafarer at the time of the great wave?"

"Yes."

"What did you see?"

"A — a bright silvery-coloured object which looked like a
small boat."

"Where did it come from?"

That was the first time she had asked herself that question —
and Palfrey hadn't asked it, either. Where *had* it come from?
She felt a moment of panic, and her breathing became shallow.

She said: "I didn't see, but——"

"Go on."

"I assumed it came out of the sea."

Out of the sea.

"Did you tell Palfrey that?"

She didn't answer.

The Patriarch waved his hand in an imperious gesture
which seemed to hint at anger as well as impatience, but above
everything there was authority; this man had only to wave his
hand, and he was obeyed.

Julia wanted to cry out: "No! I'll tell you everything." She wanted to brace herself against the pressure of Boris's arm. She did neither, but stood silent and unaided. The Patriarch looked down at papers on his desk, and appeared to forget her existence: it was as if she no longer mattered.

The two guards moved. Boris raised his left hand in that casual way. Another door opened. Julia was half pushed through; Boris obviously expected her to resist and was surprised when she did not. She stumbled.

"I am sorry," Boris said.

"It's all right."

"I told you," he said.

He had meant: "I am sorry about what is going to happen."

"I know."

"Julia, please understand this. There are two stages of the — the Suffering. It is used on everyone who comes here but who is not one of us. After the first stage, you must give way. You will have an opportunity, and must take it. The second stage has been known to send men mad."

Julia did not answer. She felt cold, and little shivers went up and down her spine. There were tremors at her legs and arms, too. The impulse to give way now was almost overwhelming, she was so frightened.

She began: "Boris, please——"

He took no notice.

"Please——"

He raised his hand at another door. It slid open. As it did so, a great wave seemed to rise up in front of her, like the wave she had seen from the deck of the *Seafarer*. She cowered back, and banged against something hard. She twisted round, screaming:

"Boris!"

He was not there. Behind her there was only a blank wall.

"No!" she gasped. "No!"

She was robbed of all reason and rational thought as she saw a great mountain of green water, filled with millions of iridescent lights. She heard the hissing roar which had come when the wave had struck the ship. She felt the sharp, hard pellets of spray. The wave was so close that it was bound to swallow her up, so close that she had no chance to save herself. With a futile gesture she thrust her hands forward, as if to fend the great wave off.

It stopped.

She stood there in shivering terror.

15

ORDEAL BY TEMPEST

In the few seconds which followed, there was absolute stillness about Julia. Her mind was so keyed to terror that she could not think, could only feel.

In front of her the sea whirled and tossed, towering above her head yet never coming really close. Great waves seemed to smash into one another in a seething tempest. The wind howled and roared, but did not touch her. It had all the vivid horror of a nightmare — but it had reality, too, hideous reality.

She cowered back against the wall behind her, fought for breath, kept telling herself to think, think, *think*.

The Patriarch was trying to terrify her into talking, but what about? She couldn't remember. All this fear, and she could not remember. *Think*. It would not come back to her mind, but — Boris had told her there would be a respite. There were two stages in — what had he called it? *The Suffering*. This was the first stage, and the second could drive men mad. Was it *all*? Would she now get her second chance?

Think.

Boris had vanished; where there had been a passage, there was a wall of steel. How had it happened? It was like some devilish magic.

What a fool she was! A door had slid across the passage behind her; that was all. It had moved silently, like all the doors here. There was no sound.

There was no sound here now.

She stared, transfixed, at the heaving, whirling, silent waves. No, that couldn't be right. There could be no such fury of movement without sound. It was like a television picture with sound cut off: like looking at a film without a sound track. Remember that. It was like——

It was like the ordeal by light and sound to which Palfrey had subjected her, years ago, in order to test her nerve. Now she remembered that, and became much calmer. This *was* unreal, a film of some kind.

Sound smashed down and from all sides. The tumultuous waves seemed to come at her from right and left and from in front of her, as well as from above. Those hail-like pellets of spray smacked into her face, her body, her hands and arms and legs, each piece causing agony. The roar of the seas smashed at her again. She felt as if she were being drawn into the water. Desperately she tried to remind herself that it was a picture, the noise was coming out of loud speakers, tuned to deafening volume. She thrust her hands over her ears to try to keep out the sound. It was a picture. *Oh, dear God, it was a picture.* But the spray, these bullet-like pellets of water which thrashed her — they were real, pain was real, but — *it was a picture.* Remember, it was——

Water smashed down and engulfed her.

In an awful moment she was floundering helplessly, arms and legs working. She took in a great gulp of water, so noisomely salt that she was sick. With the retching, she swallowed more water. There was the awful noise, the hissing, the water tossing her about, the water in her stomach and in her lungs. One moment it was dark. The next, lights flashed in her eyes, lights which seemed to come from within as well as from outside. She was hurled about until her senses ebbed away, and she was aware only of furious throbbing in her head and ceaseless pressure against her lungs.

She lost consciousness.

When she began to come round, it was pitch dark. On the moment of waking she was filled with a kind of palpitating fear which comes upon one in a nightmare. She lay rigid. Her body felt as if she had been beaten savagely. Every part of her ached so badly that she knew she would cry out in agony if she moved; so, she dare not move.

She remembered what had led to all this.

She thought: *Is this death?*

She was aware of wet clothes, of water splashing about her, cold and slimy. It was as if she was lying in a huge bath, with a few inches of water in it, which splashed against moving sides. She heard the soft lapping of the water, the gentle sounds as it went lazily from side to side.

Then, she became aware of light. It was very dim at first, but unmistakably an easing of the awful blackness. Soon, she was able to make out the water where it splashed against the walls, and fell back.

Gradually, the light brightened.

She ventured to move. Her body still ached, but without the agony she had expected. She moved again. Her arms, legs and face were hot, as if flushed from the flailing of those pellets of spray; it was rather as though she had been burned and her body, especially that part exposed to the water, was stinging terribly.

The light grew still brighter.

Now she could see that she was indeed lying in water, which was only an inch or two deep. She turned her head. Where the waves had built up to the fury of that storm, the sea was calm. She stared at it, as she might from a ship which was low in the water. This was heavy, green sea, with hardly a wave but an ugly swell.

Slowly, she came to realise that the water was escaping. There was none left, only a wet floor. Beyond this room the sea writhed in a fury of violence; that was all.

Then Boris said: "Come, Julia."

He appeared in front of her. He came forward and helped her first to her knees, then to her feet. She felt too dizzy to stand, and would have fallen but for his support. She leaned on him heavily as they went towards the end of a passage. She did not see him give the casual wave of his hand, but in a moment the two guards appeared. Boris helped her through the narrow doorway, and into the recess where the Patriarch had been.

He was still there.

He looked up, and said: "Let her stand by herself."

She wanted to cry out: "I can't stand!"

Boris took his arm away. She swayed, trying desperately to save herself, but could not. She fell heavily, banging her right arm and knee. Her whole body was burning, and with this additional pain there was the indignity of helplessness. She gritted her teeth as she tried to get up unaided. Twice she reached her knees; each time, she collapsed.

Boris was behind her; the Patriarch was sitting and staring at her, as if commanding her to get up.

Or did he want her to grovel?

As the thought entered her head, she realised that she *was* grovelling.

She fought for strength, and managed to get to her feet. The Patriarch did not speak. She swayed first from side to side, then, in a supreme effort to steady herself, swayed to and fro. By some effort of will, she righted herself, and stood in front of the desk, swaying much less than she had.

The Patriarch asked:

"Did you tell Palfrey that you actually saw this silvery vessel rise out of the sea?"

*   *   *

That was the question she had refused to answer, of course; she remembered that vividly now. That had been the cause of her ordeal. She remembered other things; among them, that Boris had almost pleaded with her to give in after the first stage in "the Suffering".

She wondered what Palfrey would want her to do.

She felt as if the floor was giving way beneath her, and lurched forward. It was the same kind of movement she had felt in the other room, and it brought back the horror of that experience. As she flung out her arms to save herself, she realised that she was standing on a section of the floor which rocked wildly. The Patriarch's desk was quite steady; so was the man himself, as he sat watching her as if willing her to give way.

Slowly, the rocking stopped. Every muscle in Julia's body ached and burned, and she did not think she could stand any more of this treatment. How could she be sure what Palfrey would want her to do? How could she be sure that the issue on which she had taken her stand was important?

The Patriarch said: "I will ask you once more. Did you tell Palfrey that you saw the silver vessel rise *out* of the sea?"

She said hoarsely: "No. No, I didn't."

From that moment on, she felt that she hated this man, because of what he had done to her, and because he had imposed his will upon her — and because he smiled, now, with insufferable superiority.

"Now tell me what you did tell him," he ordered.

She obeyed, hating herself all the time, fearful in case she was harming Palfrey and the work he was trying to do; not absolutely sure that she was doing the wrong thing, but fearing it.

When she had finished, the Patriarch said to Boris: "Let her sleep."

Boris touched her arm. She turned, and went out with him, as in a daze. Once they had stepped through the doorway and the guards were behind them, Boris said:

"You will be all right now."

Julia did not speak.

"We will go upstairs."

Boris raised his right arm, and a small doorway opened, to reveal a small lift. There was only just room for them together, and their bodies touched. He seemed oblivious, staring over her head all the time. The lift stopped without any jolt, and Boris stepped out first.

This was another long, narrow passage, with glass walls. As

she followed him along it, she glanced to the right, and almost stopped in her tracks. Beyond the glass wall were rows and rows of beds. It was like a huge hospital ward, except that the beds were so close together — four, no *five* rows of them, with at least thirty beds in each row.

In each, a person was sleeping.

Some were men; some were women. All were wearing the uniform dress which was all she had seen here. Each was lying on his or her back, legs close together, arms by the sides — like an army felled, while standing at attention.

There was not a movement in them.

She could hardly bring herself to turn her head and look in the other direction.

It was utterly fantastic.

There was a huge swimming bath, with diving boards, both high and low, with chairs and tables, *with beach umbrellas* — and it seemed as if she were looking at some sunlit lido. Men and women were swimming, or bathing, or lazing. Some wore clothes, but everyone in the calm water was naked. The swimmers moved about with supreme ease and confidence; more like porpoises than like human beings. Some were smiling.

Julia realised then as she had before, that all of these people were of the same age. The only "old man" whom she had seen here was the Patriarch.

All this time, she followed Boris.

"First you will sleep," he declared. "Then you will take the waters."

She did not want to sleep, the thought of being one among those rows and rows of mummies terrified her.

"Boris," she protested in a gasping voice, "I don't want——"

"Julia, you should realise by now that what you want is unimportant. What *he* wants is the only thing that matters. Now you are going to sleep. You will need a 3 grain injection of *hypnotin* for the first sleep, 2 grains for the second, and thereafter 1 grain until you are able to induce the sleep yourself. You will suffer no ill-effects. You will simply sink into a coma and remain in that comatose state for a period. You will wake feeling better than you have ever felt in your life."

She ought to fight against — what did he call it? — *hypnotin.* But her body burned and ached, her mind was bemused, and she had already known too much of the result of defying the Patriarch, the man whose word was law.

The hatred for him surged up in her.

She thought: If I ever get back I will be able to tell Palfrey the silliest story he's ever heard——

Silliest?

She giggled.

She was worn out, of course, exhausted, suffering from a nervous condition which could soon lead to hysteria. Perhaps it was as well that they were going to put her to sleep.

She felt a sharp pain in her arm, just above the elbow.

Boris smiled at her, as at a child.

"You will be all right," he assured her. "You will be much better when you come round, and before long you will like being here."

He led her to a small recess off the big dormitory, where those mummies "slept". She glanced at them, touched again with horror, but it was not long lived. Boris pointed to a single bed, narrow enough for a bunk in the "cabin" where she had first woken. She got onto it, already feeling tired — and less frightened. She lay down. He bent over her, and pulled one of the lightweight sheets over her, and immediately went away. The light was a soothing pearly glow which did not dazzle or trouble her. She lay, drowsily, recalling all that had happened, but her thoughts were vague and hazy, as if her mind was filled with mist.

Then she thought: What did Boris mean — "before long you will like it here?"

Did he expect her to stay?

That brought her the first moment of real panic since the injection, but she was so drowsy that it soon faded. Her body seemed atrophied, as if she could not stir a muscle, and life was being drained out of her. Then a gentle whisper came to her ears, soft, insidious, repeated over and over again:

"*When you wake you will obey the Patriarch. When you wake you will obey the Patriarch. When you wake . . .*"

16

LIVING DEATH

"SHE looks like death," Dr Ephraim Higgins said to Palfrey. "Her heart is beating so slowly that if she were a normal human being I would say that she would not live the day out. I have seen cases similar in some ways, although none exactly the same. I remember a young woman who had lost her husband and twin children in an accident. She surrendered the will to live. Her life gradually ebbed away. She looked less healthy than this young woman, but apart from that the similarity is most marked." Higgins stopped, looked at Palfrey across the single bed on which Leah lay, and asked flatly: "Who is she?"

Palfrey said: "We don't know. Is she normal in all other respects?"

Higgins echoed: "*Normal?*"

He was a short, very stocky man. His exceptional breadth of shoulder made him look even shorter than his five feet four, and he had a short, thick neck. His chin was like a spade, thrusting downwards aggressively. He had small, buried, periwinkle blue eyes. His iron grey hair, with three crowns, stuck up in several different directions, and was smoothed down only at the front, obviously the result of vigorous, long term brushing. His face was brick red, like that of a man who spent much of his time at sea or on the open moorlands or the high mountains.

"Yes," Palfrey said. "Normal."

"Shouldn't think there's anything abnormal, except in her condition," answered Higgins. "Except——"

"What?"

"Perfection isn't normal."

"Ah," said Palfrey.

"Most beautifully proportioned woman I've seen for a long time."

"Physically?"

"Of course. Hands, arms, legs, bosom——" Higgins pulled the sheet right off and continued his clinical assessment. "Look at those fingers, and the nails. *Perfect*. Help me to make her sit up." Palfrey did so. "See the fall of those breasts — the contours. *Perfect*. The colour of the skin, the brown of the nipples. And look — the shape of the lips, nose, eyes——"

"I've got the point," Palfrey said.

"So I should hope."

"Blemishless, in other words."

"Yes. That skin — do you know, Palfrey, I haven't seen skin like it except——"

"Well?"

"One or two Oriental races," Higgins answered. "Spent a lot of time in the Far East, you know. The occasional truly pure race with no contamination of blood, is still found."

"Pure?"

"You know what I mean."

"I don't."

"Then you should." Higgins pulled at the lobe of his right ear. "Let me put it this way. Some people, in parts of Australia and in the United States, in South America and some little known parts of the Orient, have perfect teeth; calcium in the water is the secret. Even skeletons found hundreds of years after burial have no sign of decay in the teeth. In other places, the local conditions — water, soil, even air — create other perfections. Some people have remarkable eyesight, others exceptional hair — as in some Balkan countries — others very powerful muscles, others a skin free from blemish. This girl has — but damn it, Palfrey! You know all this as well as I do!"

Palfrey was playing with his hair.

"Part of it," he admitted. "As far as you can judge, this girl is a perfect physical specimen."

"Yes."

"In spite of the coma."

Higgins ran all of his fingers through his hair.

"Conceivably because of it."

"Ah," said Palfrey.

"Suspected that, did you?"

"I had an uneasy suspicion," Palfrey admitted.

"Uneasy? Suspicion? What's the matter with you?"

"The cost of perfection could be too high," Palfrey said. "Mind looking at another corpse?"

"Must I?"

"Please."

"Very well," Higgins agreed. "But Palfrey, you know what this might be, don't you?"

"Yes."

"Prove that you know."

"A variation of deep-freeze," Palfrey answered. "Coma with very slow heart beat. Absolute rest; if one has enough of it, it could prolong life for a long time."

"Indefinitely," Higgins said. "Indefinitely. Some recent experiments have shown beyond doubt that if the strength and functions of the heart can be maintained over a long enough period by complete rest, the other parts of the body will remain healthy for a very long time. Centuries. Methorst in his experiments in Vienna, Grundig in Frankfurt, Balmain in Chicago, Mitsni in Tokyo, are all working along those lines, and animals with a normal life expectancy of three years have lived to ten. Comparatively few experiments, *as far as we know*" — Higgins paused for the significance of that proviso to sink in — "have been made with human beings. However, this woman——"

"How old is she?"

"Don't ask me to guess."

"Guess."

"Between twenty and forty-five."

Palfrey said: "I see." They were walking along passages in

the shelter, watched curiously by the guards, for they made such a strange contrast, with Palfrey towering over Higgins, and Higgins looking twice as broad across the shoulders.

They went into a small, cold room. On a stone bench lay a draped figure. Palfrey pulled the white sheet down, over the naked body of the man who had been found at the bottom of the ravine in the mountains. There were no signs of decomposition. The legs and arms were badly bruised and there were other ugly bruises at the neck and chest. Apart from these and the broken arm the body looked to be in perfect condition, and the skin was almost identical with the colour, texture and blemishlessness of the girl Leah's.

Higgins caught his breath, and bent over the body.

Soon, he drew back.

"Everything I said about the girl is true of this man. How did he die?"

"Of a broken neck, presumably from a fall."

"When?"

"Forty-eight hours ago."

"Has there been any embalming?"

"None. The body has been kept in this temperature."

"Palfrey," Higgins said in a throaty voice, "you're onto something quite remarkable here."

"Phenomenal?"

"Undoubtedly."

"That's what I was afraid of."

"*Afraid?*" Higgins's eyes were glistening, his big strong hands waved excitedly, he began to stamp about the room. "Palfrey, this could be the secret which man has been seeking since the dawn of humankind. This might be the secret of extending the physical life span beyond man's dreams. This might be——" Higgins broke off, almost choking. "My God! Don't *you* see?"

"I see," Palfrey said. He patted the tendrils of hair down into a little kiss-curl, having no idea how quaint the mannerism looked, and then went on: "I want to know the price."

"It is priceless. *Beyond* all price."

"Not yet," Palfrey objected.

"Are you *mad*?"

"Possibly," Palfrey said. "Before we can live for so long I would like to see a better kind of man with a dream of absolute goodness. You know what happened in Nice. You know——"

"Oh, sentimental bosh!" exclaimed Higgins. "You, a scientist, ought to know better."

"A human being."

"Now, Palfrey! I'm disappointed in you. You're a scientist first. This could be mankind's dream. To save what we have called peace and freedom and liberty, all the human rights, we have fought savage wars and killed millions — hundreds of millions! — of people. A localised disaster like that at Nice — come! Before this year is out there will be a dozen natural disasters causing as much or more in suffering and destruction — and all purposeless. Understand? All without purpose of any kind. But this — my God, Palfrey, you ought to be crying for joy. Can you find where these people come from? Can you even——?"

He broke off.

Palfrey turned his head. The door had opened some seconds before and he had seen who it was out of the corner of his eye. Higgins had been so transported by his reactions that he had noticed nothing. Now he turned, also.

A giant came in, a man so broad, so tall, so massive in every way, that he made Higgins gape, seemed to drive away all the excitement in the doctor. The giant closed the door. His movements were slow and deliberate, as if he knew that a man of such size and such physical development had to use his strength with care. He was neither dark nor fair, and his wiry hair, brushed straight back from his forehead, waved slightly. He was handsome, and the size of his features did nothing to detract from that handsomeness. His eyes were a clear grey, and the expression was one of great calmness.

Looking at him, it would be easy to believe that one was looking at the face of a saint.

He smiled.

"Hallo, Sap."

"Hallo, Stefan." Palfrey touched Higgins' arm. "You haven't met Dr Ephraim Higgins, have you? Higgins — here's Stefan Andromovitch, who works with me."

The Russian stood head and shoulders above Higgins.

"My God!" Higgins gasped. "They come in King Size, too."

Palfrey smiled. Andromovitch put out his hand. Higgins hesitated before he took it.

"I am honoured," Andromovitch said.

"I'm bewildered," said Higgins. "First Palfrey shocks me with longevity, then——"

"Did you hear us?" Palfrey asked Andromovitch.

"Yes."

"Then tell him how right I am," urged Higgins. "Tell him that this is the greatest discovery yet made by man. If you know where these two came from, you've got to tell the world. The scientific world, anyhow. The fact that he appears to have shown his power by a demonstration like that at Nice isn't important. No one could overcome men like *these*."

Andromovitch said: "I imagine a lot of people will think like you."

"Don't you agree?"

"No."

"*Two* lunatics!"

"Dr Higgins," Andromovitch said in his calm voice, "Palfrey is quite right. When we have found absolute goodness we can start to concern ourselves about finding everlasting or absolute life — not until then."

"This is humanitarian hogwash."

"Sap," Andromovitch said, "I have just come back via London, as you know."

"Yes."

"Merritt has had the replies in from over a hundred agents, since we described this woman. There are seventeen authenticated instances of this kind of human being having been found, always in a coma. The reports come from hospitals and clinics. Most of the people have come round, but given no satisfactory explanation of their condition. Only a few can be traced."

"*Seventeen* of them!" cried Higgins. "These aren't isolated cases, then. If anyone can do this seventeen times, it *is* the greatest discovery mankind has ever made."

"All right," Palfrey said. "If it's what we think it is, it's a great discovery——"

"The greatest!"

"We still have to compute the price paid for it."

"No price could be too high. Palfrey — I want to have this woman examined by Smythe-Paterson. I want to take her to London. Quickly."

"Well, you can't," Palfrey said. "You can have the man's body flown over, if you want, for an autopsy, but not the woman's. Stefan — where did the reports come from?"

"I am quoting Merritt," Stefan answered. "Two come from Japan, one from Australia, one from Germany, two from Russia, one——" as he went on, Higgins began to pace the room, as if he could not keep still.

"Whom are the reports from?"

"Our own agents. They've followed the request we sent out on the day of the wave at Nice for more information about the investigations into the disappearance of scientists. We sent a description of the woman's physical condition and used the phrase 'self-hypnosis'. In three cases the suspects are known to have been spying on our own investigators — in each case the suspects escaped. One of them was killed in a car smash soon afterwards, and the pathologist's report made it clear that——"

"Where can I see the report?" interrupted Higgins. "I need to see it."

"We'll make it available for you," Palfrey promised. "What about the other fourteen, Stefan?"

The giant spread his great hands, and answered:

"They all corresponded to the description of the woman Leah. The common factor in each case was the golden-coloured skin, absolutely free from blemish. In five cases after men were questioned they went into a coma which seemed to be faked. Only since our inquiry has self-hypnosis been considered. In some cases the suspect recovered and swam out to sea and was lost, or jumped overboard from a ship or even parachuted from aircraft into the sea."

Stefan stopped.

"Do you mean they disappeared beneath the water and haven't come back?" squeaked Higgins.

"That is exactly what I mean. Many of these suspects disappeared in much the same way as Professor Corvell, and as many other scientists and specialists of renown."

"Into the *sea*," breathed Higgins. "Do you think that's where they come from?" Before either of the others could speak, he answered himself. "Of course not. It's ludicrous. They must have been taken away by fast moving craft. They must have been." He caught his breath. "We've got to find one of them, got to make them talk. Palfrey, I still don't think you understand the breathtaking significance of this. It could alter the course of mankind's history."

Palfrey said gravely: "At least we're agreed on that. New——"

He stopped when there was a tap at the door of the room. Duval came in, on Palfrey's call.

"Dr Palfrey," he said. "There is a message for you. A message of great importance." He glanced at Higgins, hesitated, and went on in a flat voice: "From the man who caused so much destruction in Nice."

17

SECOND ULTIMATUM

HIGGINS stared open-mouthed. Andromovitch hardly stirred.

"What is the message?" Palfrey asked.

"He is to telephone you at four o'clock." Duval glanced at his watch, and the others instinctively did the same; it was now twenty minutes to four. "Will you talk to him?"

"Yes."

"Thank you."

"Does he know where I am?"

"The message was received from the Chief of Police at Nice. You were asked to be at a telephone in the Nice region, at four o'clock."

"Will it do here?"

"Yes. When the call comes it will be put through to any number you wish."

"We'll go to the office," Palfrey said. "Will you find out——" he hesitated. "I'll talk to Merritt," he said, and went briskly to the door. "We need to make every effort to find out where this man calls from. If it's humanly possible to trace that call——"

He broke off.

"Palfrey," Higgins said, "it *must* be traced. You've got to do a deal with this man. *I've* got to talk to him. If I had ten minutes with him, five even, I might get a clue to the secret."

"I'll do all I can," Palfrey assured him.

In the age of easy communications, he was talking to Merritt in London within three minutes. Duval was with him, but Higgins was out of the office when the call came through.

"You've seen Stefan, I hope," Merritt said.

"Yes, I have. Alec, I want you to send immediate radio-communication to every agent. A call is coming to me at Nice from an unknown source. I must trace it. If ordinary communications are used——"

Merritt said: "They won't be."

"Why not?"

"He's talked to me," Merritt answered, bleakly. "He uses radio-telephonic methods, breaking in on one of our usual wave-lengths as and when he pleases. No one has yet been able to trace the source of the call. Sap——"

"Yes."

"He has threatened to destroy all the capital ships of the British Navy unless you release the woman Leah."

*   *   *

Palfrey stood quite still, with his hand on the telephone. Duval shifted his position. After a long pause, Alec Merritt asked:

"Are you there, Sap?"

"Yes."

"Do you think he can do it?"

"I hope we don't have to find out."

"Sap."

"Yes?"

"The *British* Navy."

"I know," Palfrey said. "The real test of loyalty — to Z5 or to Great Britain. He's as cunning as he's powerful, but——"

"But what?"

Palfrey answered in a puzzled voice: "*Naïve?*"

"*This* devil?"

"Isn't he? Cunning but simple and direct. No subtlety."

Slowly, Merritt said: "I see what you mean. I shouldn't place much reliance on that."

"I won't, but it's worth remembering. Simple, direct and without subtlety, he works on the assumption that force will always get him what he wants."

"Perhaps it will."

"We'll see," Palfrey said. "We'll see. Anything in since Stefan left?"

"Not a great deal," answered Merritt. "Some confirmation that suspects have often vanished at sea."

"Under the sea."

"What are you driving at?" demanded Merritt.

Palfrey glanced at Duval, and said slowly: "The freak waves start from beneath the sea. The men and women vanish under or into the sea. There is now this threat to the British Navy."

"A great sea power, you mean?"

"It could be," Palfrey agreed, non-committally. "Is there any news of Garri-Garri?"

"Not really news," answered Merritt. "I've had interim reports from Peverill and Marchesi, in New York. Garri-Garri had done more work than anyone else on extending the human life span. He kept going off into little known places looking for remote tribes, anything and anyone which would help him to get nearer the secret. Ten years ago he talked of being very near. Then he stopped making claims and went on with his researches. It was said——"

"That he'd had two or three bad failures, and didn't propose to make any more statements until he could prove his theories. He boasted that he could add twenty years to the normal human life span." Everything Palfrey had ever heard about Garri-Garri poured into his mind. "As a Hindu he was brought up to believe in reincarnation, to seeing death as a stepping stone to another, better life. In the higher castes — among the Brahmins particularly, there is less promise of improvement, and more desire for longevity."

Palfrey stopped.

"Sap," Merritt said. "He disappeared off the coast of Portugal."

The memory was still vivid in Palfrey's mind when he waited for the call to come through at the offices of the shelter. Stefan and Duval were in a small listening-room, into which any conversation could be relayed. They would hear every word.

Throughout the world, Z5 agents, the regular police forces, the secret services of a hundred nations, were alert for the coming call.

The telephone bell rang.

Palfrey started. Stefan raised one hand. Palfrey moved towards the instrument and lifted it.

"This is Dr Palfrey," he said very clearly.

"Dr Palfrey," a man replied. "I trust you received my message."

"Your message," Palfrey echoed, and to those who did not know him he would have sounded vague. "Now let me see——"

"I am not here to play." The voice sharpened.

"I'm sure you're not," Palfrey said. "Just to joke."

"*Joke?* You will find out if I'm joking."

"No one would threaten the British Navy *except* as a joke."

"Dr Palfrey," the man said, "you are to release Leah. She is to be placed in a motor boat, and the boat must be headed towards the spot where the *Seafarer* was struck at a speed of fifteen knots. There must be no pilot, no watching aircraft, no pursuing vessels. This must begin at five o'clock tomorrow morning. If you have not obeyed, then by noon tomorrow Britain will not have a single ship over 1,000 tons afloat. *And I am not joking.*"

"Oh," Palfrey said, mildly. His hand strayed to his hair. "That's a pity."

"I tell you——"

"Shall I say good-bye to Leah for you?"

"What do you mean?"

"I mean that if a single ship of any navy is sunk, I will choke the life out of Leah with my own hands," Palfrey said. "And she's such an attractive girl. Good-bye."

"Palfrey!"

"I have a lot to do," Palfrey said. "Good-bye."

"*Do not kill Leah.*"

"I won't harm her at all provided you don't carry out your threats," Palfrey said. "It's as simple as that."

He took the receiver from his ear, hesitated, then put it down slowly. His lips were set in a thin line. His eyes were narrowed, and he stared at Stefan as if he could not see him. There was a beading of sweat on his forehead and his upper lip, and he was deathly pale.

"Sap, you were right," Stefan said quickly.

"You think so?" Palfrey's eyes nearly closed.

"I'm sure. If he was so anxious to save this Leah that he would use the Nice wave as a terror-weapon, he wants her desperately. If he believes you will kill her——"

"Ah. Did I convince him?"

"I think so."

"I wouldn't like to say," Palfrey said. "He must know I'm as anxious that he shouldn't touch the Navy as he is that Leah shouldn't come to any harm. Stefan" — he stretched out and touched the big man's arm — "he can, you know. That's the dreadful thing. He *can* destroy the ships. I don't need any convincing."

Stefan said: "I don't, either."

Palfrey began to move about the room.

"We know he can do it, so — what else can he do?"

"He can control the seas."

"And anyone in control of the sea can control the land," reasoned Palfrey simply. "*Polaris* is the deadliest weapon yet known to man because it cannot be sought out and destroyed beneath the water." The sweat was still on Palfrey's forehead, and heavier on his lips. "Stefan, if we don't get this man, if we don't stop him — it will be our fault."

"No, Sap——"

"It will be our fault," Palfrey interrupted roughly. "We knew about the disappearances of the athletes from ships coming back from the Olympic Games, we knew about the disappearance of the *Medici* with sixty of the world's best scientific brains on board, and then *Venus of Milo*, and about the individual disappearances *over the years*. We never looked beneath the sea for a malicious cause. How blind can men be?"

"Sap," Stefan said, "we're looking there now."

"When it might be too late."

Stefan said, sharply for him: "What's got into you? Why don't you stop crying over spilt milk? You handled the man as if you had all the confidence in the world. Go on working, not reproaching yourself."

There was a moment of silence. Palfrey was about to speak when the telephone bell rang. He started again, a sure indication of his raw nerves. Stefan did not look away.

Palfrey picked up the receiver.

"Palfrey."

"We traced that call," Alec Merritt told him. "It came from a ship in mid-Atlantic, relayed by radio telephone. It was beyond the range of aircraft. Ships in the vicinity have been asked to keep a look out, but——"

Merritt paused.

"Go on," Palfrey's voice was taut, as if with anger.

"I've checked with the Navy. The position of the ship from which the call came is not on any normal shipping lines. No large vessels are known to be in the area at all. It's almost as if this came from a submarine. As if it surfaced to make the call."

"I see," Palfrey said. "Thanks, Alec."

"Sap."

"Yes?"

"The whole world heard what he said."

"That part of the world that matters," Palfrey agreed.

"Sap."

"For God's sake don't go on saying 'Sap'!"

"I can imagine how you feel," Merritt said. "You probably see the implications better than I do."

"Spell them out for me," Palfrey said stiffly.

"The Admiralty heard that threat," said Merritt. "The Admiralty doesn't want to lose its ships. They don't know why this woman Leah is so important."

"I know it," Palfrey said. "But does anyone else?"

"The Admiralty has referred to Downing Street. Downing Street has called a meeting of the Ambassadors of the member countries of Z5," Merritt went on. "They want you here, at midnight."

"I see," said Palfrey, and after a pause: "I'll be there."

*   *   *

Stefan, who heard the conversation on the extension telephone, put down his receiver at the same time as Palfrey. Stefan spoke first, in a gentle voice:

"How strong is your case, Sap?"

"By ordinary standards, not strong at all."

"Could you justify taking the risk?"

"I can *feel* justified," Palfrey said. "It's a fifty-fifty chance whether he will believe I will actually kill Leah."

"Will you?"

"I would have to," Palfrey said. "If he forces this issue and I don't kill the girl, then I will never have any hope of fighting him."

He broke off at a sharp tap at the door, and added: "This will be Duval." He called: "Come in."

The door was thrust open by a young captain, with Duval immediately behind him. Palfrey could judge from the expression on Duval's face that the news was bad. He forced a smile when the captain drew himself up, and saluted.

"Dr Palfrey, I have instructions to escort you to an aircraft which will take you to London. M'sieu Andromovitch, there will be a seat on the plane for you, also."

"So they mean it," Palfrey said, gruffly.

"Dr Palfrey," Duval said. "The authorities here have taken the woman Leah from her room, and have refused to tell me where she can be found."

"That is so," the captain said. "She is in our custody, Dr Palfrey. We shall take care of her until instructions are received from Paris."

*   *   *

"They mean to make sure I can't harm her," Palfrey said bleakly to Stefan. "They don't think I'm a good risk."

18

S.I.B.

PALFREY stepped into the conference room in the underground headquarters of Z5 in London. Joyce Morgan was
sitting at a small table near the door, with a list in front of her,
ticking off the names of the representatives who came from the
different member countries. The Secretary-General, looking
almost severe with his pale face and close-cropped fair hair,
sat on a dais with the year's President of the Supreme International Body — known to those within the organisation as
S.I.B. Next to Merritt on the other side was Ivan Tarov, the
Russian Ambassador. On the President's other side was
Geoffrey Mandell, the special envoy of the President of the
United States. These two men were very much alike physically,
heavy-featured, dark-haired, rather solemn, even earnest. To
look at, they might be expected to be at each other's throats
at every opportunity. In fact they worked well together, particularly in S.I.B. The President was Le Blum, of Belgium,
short, dapper, with black waxed moustache and black waxed
beard — and very dark clearly defined eyebrows.

Palfrey paused by Joyce's table.

"Hallo, Joyce. What can you tell me?"

"They're very worried," Joyce said.

"The understatement of the year!" Palfrey smiled vaguely
and went along to the desks which were in the well of the
conference room. He sat down. No one else was there, but as
the red upholstered seats filled up, one by one, Stefan came
and joined him. There had always been and there would
always be a bond between these two men; when the Russian
was at hand, Palfrey always felt more sure of himself. Now, he
played with his hair as he said:

"Anyone been getting at you?"

Stefan smiled. "Tarov, of course, and Mandell."

"Together?"

"Separately. Each really wants to know the same thing."

"What?"

"Has Dr Palfrey taken leave of his senses?"

"Am I mad?" Palfrey said. "Sometimes I think I am." He looked round as the President said: "Will we need that?" Behind him was a small movie projector, so that a picture could be thrown on a screen which was visible to everyone present. "Or are they the mad ones?"

Stefan made no comment.

So far, Palfrey reminded himself, Stefan had made no commitment about his own views. He would be questioned by the delegates, as would Palfrey, and he would say what he believed — friendship would not influence him in any way. Was there any significance in the fact that he had not yet given his opinion?

Merritt called: "Is everyone here, Miss Morgan?"

"Yes, Mr Secretary."

"Are the doors sealed?"

"Yes, Mr Secretary."

"Mr President," the Secretary-General said in a clear aside, "the session may open when you wish."

To Palfrey it was like a court scene in a film or on the stage. The half circle of "judges", the dapper President and his attendants on the dais, he and Stefan down here — he had been through this a dozen, a hundred times before, although never in such circumstances, never with the realisation that the mood of the delegates was almost entirely antagonistic.

"Gentlemen," the President began, "we have been summoned to consider a crisis of extreme urgency. We know the background situation. We have convincing evidence that many disappearances at sea have been due to the activities of one man, whose name we do not yet know. We have positive evidence that he is able to create extremely dangerous conditions throughout the oceans of the world. We know, from reports and photographs received during the past twenty-four hours, what he was able to do on the French Riviera." There was a pause, then the lights dimmed, and some photographs were flashed onto the screen. The scene of destruction and disaster, the floating bodies and the broken boats showed in stark horror. "I do not think there can be one among us who is not fully aware of the danger from this individual," Le Blum went on. "Is there?"

He paused, to glance round.

Chetnic, of Poland, looked at Palfrey pointedly.

"A danger we should have known about long ago," he said.

Two or three delegates nodded.

"*Long* ago," echoed Palo, of Brazil. "Why haven't we?"

"I don't think it is the purpose of this meeting to investigate that," demurred the President. "The time may come later, but the immediate task is to decide policy for the next twelve — in fact the next four hours."

"If we know how it has been possible for this man to be so active for so long, it might be possible for us to decide the best course of action," interposed Smythe, of Great Britain.

Palfrey looked at him intently.

Smythe was one of the old school, a conventionalist in every way; it was commonly said that he had been born half a century too late. He stuck rigidly to protocol, carried out the instructions of his government to the letter, and never yielded an inch to ease any situation. There was little doubt that he had been told to press for the release of the woman Leah, as "he" had ordered; how could the British representative do any less?

"Dr Palfrey," the President said, deferring to the others, "if you have any statement to make at this stage we will be glad to hear it."

Palfrey stood up.

"None at all," he said.

"I'm not sure that is good enough," Mandell put in. "It has been happening under our noses for a long time, Mr President."

"Dr Palfrey?"

Palfrey, still standing, put his right hand to his hair.

"I've no statement to make at this juncture," he insisted.

"Surely, if the meeting requests a statement——" the President began.

"Mr President." This was Meshnon, of India, another stickler for protocol. "I have said before at these conferences that there is too great a danger in reticence. We all understand that some secrecy must be observed in the carrying out of the operative work of the organisation, but that should not be used as a shield by Dr Palfrey, or by anyone else, to hide personal failure to meet one's obligations. This is a serious, a very serious, failure. I am not convinced that the situation is as bad as we are told. I think it would be easy for us to allow ourselves to be panicked into taking the wrong action. Certainly if we require a statement, then Dr Palfrey should give it."

"I am inclined to agree." The President's beard bobbed. "Dr Palfrey, why are you reluctant to make this explanation? We are not necessarily implying that you have been incompetent, that the fault is in any way yours."

"Of course you are," Stefan interposed, in a clear, loud voice.

The President looked astonished, not only at the interruption, but also at the source of it. Stefan Andromovitch was known as the most diffident of men at such meetings. Palfrey looked startled, and glanced sideways at the giant. Tarov leaned forward, his lips compressed in a hint of an ironic smile.

"When the President is speaking——" Merritt began.

"We shall overlook that interruption," the President declared. He was like a perky little sparrow; whenever he spoke that pointed black beard wagged like a reproving finger. "I repeat, we are not necessarily implying that any of the operative staff has failed, but——"

"Mr President," Stefan interrupted in the same deep voice, "I would like your permission to retire."

He stood up, towering over Palfrey, almost as tall as the men sitting on that raised dais. He gave a stiff bow, from the waist, and turned his back on the President. The surprise was so complete that no one attempted to stop him, or even to speak, until he had reached the desk where Joyce was sitting. Then Merritt called:

"Andromovitch — please!"

Stefan turned.

"Well?"

He looked not only massive, but furiously angry. The glitter in his eyes was like the glitter of steel under harsh white lights. His arms were straight by his sides, the fists clenched.

"You are required to attend so as to give evidence and opinion."

"*Evidence?*" Stefan echoed. "*Opinion?* Here? Who is going to listen to either? You have made up your minds what you are going to do. From the moment you stepped into this room, nearly every delegate came to condemn Dr Palfrey. Since the session opened there has been nothing but insult and ingratitude to a man who — by all that is holy, a man worth ten times any one of you. The man to whom everyone here owes his existence. Have you forgotten the past? Have you completely forgotten what he has done now that you are so safe and snug — and *smug*?" His tone and his looks were scathing. "I am finished with this organisation. *Finished* for good and all."

He turned and strode towards the door, thrust it open, and stalked out.

As the door swung to behind him, the silence of consternation fell upon the big room. Palfrey leaned back in his chair, smiled faintly, and tried not to show his gratitude and his admiration. He was quite sure that Stefan had done this to shock the delegates into a different attitude; it might even succeed. He patted down a little kiss-curl, oblivious of what he was doing, and looked up at the President.

"We don't seem to have pleased Mr Andromovitch," Mandell remarked.

"It is an unforgivable outburst," Meshnon said, angrily. "Quite unforgivable."

"Was it perhaps justifiable?" Tarov inquired.

"Mr Andromovitch must be suffering under very great stress——" the Dutch delegate interpolated mildly. "Mr

President — is the same not true of Dr Palfrey? Of us all?"

"Why won't Palfrey explain *why* this situation was allowed
to develop?" demanded Smythe.

Palfrey said, mildly: "Mr President — to explain and to
present a case covering such an investigation as this would
take several hours. To prepare it so that you could pass a true
judicial judgement, would take several weeks, perhaps months.
I — ah — I think Andromovitch was angry because he feels
that this was an emergency session, and not a trial. If you
wish to put me on trial at any time, I shall not question
your authority. But I would have thought that you could find
a more appropriate time. After all, we have less than four
hours to make the decision — whether to defy this man or
whether to let him have his Leah back. I came prepared to
discuss that. I didn't resent the fact that the woman was taken
out of my custody, although that was a strong indication of
lack of trust. I didn't greatly object to being ordered here at a
moment's notice, when I could almost certainly be of more
use in Nice. But I do object to wasting time. I — ah — I
wonder if we know the reasons for the attitude adopted by so
many delegates?"

Tarov said: "What is that?"

"Please, explain yourself," urged the President.

"I know why Mr Smythe is critical," went on Palfrey. "He
is nervous of what might happen to the British Navy — what
might very well happen, too. It *could*, you know. This unknown
man can cause under-water eruptions which would sink any
vessel afloat. He can create the conditions in which there
would be no survivors. That is the cold fact of the situation.
If I were Mr Smythe, or the British Prime Minister, I would
be very worried indeed. What particular factor is worrying
everyone else? I find it very hard to believe that Mr Meshnon
is particularly perturbed about the British Navy. Have there
been other threats? Is everyone here with instructions from
his government which way to vote?"

Tarov said: "I am not."

"Mr President, I suggest we hear the case for holding the

woman — there must be a strong one, or Dr Palfrey wouldn't advocate it." That was Arthurs, of New Zealand.

"It is obvious why he advocates it," said Khavi of Egypt. "It is the only way in which he might cover his own failures. Do *I* worry about the British Navy? As an Egyptian, no. As a member of this international group — yes, of course I do. Also — the Suez Canal could be in very great danger from this man. It is our lifeline."

"So that's it," said Mandell. "It looks as if Palfrey was right, Mr President. Our motives aren't exactly pure." When he paused he looked even more like the Russian delegate. "I would like to hear Palfrey's case."

"There is no case. A whole navy, one sixth of the naval strength of the world, against one *woman*." Swartz, of South Africa, was hard-voiced, hard-eyed.

"Dr Palfrey?" said the President and glanced about him commandingly, as if to make sure that no one interrupted. "Would you reject this ultimatum?"

"Yes, sir."

"In spite of what you yourself admit might happen?"

"Yes, sir," said Palfrey. "I don't know of any other way in which we can gain time to search for the headquarters of this man. It is as simple as that. We know now that he operates from under water. We have been in urgent touch with all countries, all naval and air authorities, military and civil, to keep a sharp look out. The Russian and the American atom-powered submarines are making special searches; so are many conventional submarines. We may find an essential clue this way, but——"

"Surely we are bound to," interposed Smythe.

"I don't think so," Palfrey said. "If this headquarters were easy to find, I think we would have had some intimation from submarines before. I think we have to contend with two possibilities. First, that there are mobile submarine stations — possibly very large submarines — carrying offensive weapons developed specially to create these waves. There is no difficulty about creating such waves, provided one can be sure of controlling the effect of them, or if one doesn't care what the effect is. A wave is dangerous only to surface shipping, to harbours and to coastlines in the wave area. It is not dangerous to anything which is below, say, a hundred fathoms. The deep water of the oceans is hardly disturbed. I don't think we need concern ourselves too much with *how* these waves are created, only with the fact that we have to find where they come from and who starts them. Certainly one of two possibilities must be accepted. Either there are a number of different permanent stations from which the waves are created — we now have proof of their incidence in all of the oceans of the world — or else there is a highly mobile submarine base."

Palfrey paused again.

"Which do you think more likely?" inquired Mandell.

"I don't think I would like to guess," Palfrey said. "But if I had to, I would say that there are a large number of bases either on the sea bed, or anchored in the water——"

"Absurd," breathed Khavi.

"I don't think it is really absurd, Mr President," Palfrey said mildly. "We would have called space stations on the way to the moon and the other planets absurd a few years ago, but now they are accepted as normal. Under-water stations might be easier — in fact they would be easier to maintain. I think if we were faced with mobile stations we would have had reports of them from time to time. We have had none, except these reports of freak waves which, until very recently, we assumed were from natural causes."

He broke off.

"Have you any idea at all how many of these — ah — under-sea stations exist?" inquired the President.

"None at all, sir."

"*None*," breathed the Egyptian. "You see."

"My own view differs from Palfrey's. I would think it much more likely that we are coping with a single, highly mobile under-water vessel," said Smythe. He rubbed the side of his thin, pinched nose.

"It seems to me that the vital fact is that we can't trace

either fixed or mobile stations," observed Mandell. "And you think that by holding this woman you might be able to trace one, Palfrey. You might be able, in due course, to make her talk."

"It's the only possibility that I can see," said Palfrey.

"Is there really a chance?" inquired Smythe. "If there were, almost any sacrifice might be worthwhile, but — the British Navy remains one of our strongest sea powers. If we have to fight a new kind of sea war, the experience of British sailors, the power of British ships, are surely essential."

"You forget something," Palfrey said.

"What do I forget?"

"If this man wants to destroy any navy, he can. If it ever comes to open warfare, unless we know what he is and where he is, we will be helpless. Any conventional navy is completely powerless. Destruction will be only a matter of time. Somehow we have to find different methods to fight him with. In this case, I submit, we must use his anxiety about the woman Leah, whom I believe might be his daughter. If we release her, as he orders, then we have nothing left to fight with except conventional forces. I don't think he will risk losing her. I think he believes me when I say that if he destroys the Navy, I will kill her with my own hands." Palfrey wiped his hand across his wet forehead as he went on: "That is the chance I think we ought to take. It depends what is the more important thing to him: this woman, alive, or victory over us. I think she is very important. I think she is the one contact we have with him, the one person who *might* be able to lead us to him.

"So, I feel sure we ought to hold her."

After a long pause, a man asked: "*Would* you kill her, Palfrey?"

Palfrey said: "It has always been agreed that the tactics should be left to me. I hope it will stay that way. Unless, of course, you have lost confidence in me completely."

"Do you mean you regard this as a vote of confidence?" asked Merritt, uneasily.

"Of course I do. If you let that woman go, I believe you

throw away the only chance we have. I would make any sacrifice to keep the chance." Palfrey shrugged his shoulders as he looked round. "Don't you see it as a vote of confidence?"

The President raised his hand, and said:

"I think you had best retire, Dr Palfrey. We will discuss this, and recall you soon."

"I hope so," Palfrey said. "We've been talking for three quarters of an hour — we have little more than three hours left."

19

DECISION

STEFAN ANDROMOVITCH was sitting in Palfrey's office, studying the charts on the wall. Many more marks had been placed on these charts since Palfrey had been in France. More reports were coming in every hour. Palfrey went to a corner cupboard, poured himself a brandy and water, and tossed it down. Stefan would not drink spirits — the only alcohol he ever touched was wine with his evening meal.

He looked round.

"Have they made their decision?"

"They've been two hours trying to," said Palfrey. "Stefan——"

"Yes?"

"Thank you."

"Sometimes I think that we have learned nothing," said Stefan. His cheeks were pale, obviously he was still angry. "To argue and bicker about national interests — do you think that 'he' has sent threats to individual countries?"

"It wouldn't surprise me."

"Sap — *have* we a chance?"

In that brief question there was a world of doubts and fears.

"We don't yet know what the man wants," he said. "If you mean have we a chance of locating him if we let Leah go — I don't see one. Has anything come in to help?"

"Nothing."

"There's one thing we have to admit," Palfrey said, heavily. "This man has fooled us for a long time." He began to walk about the office. "The one hope I see is holding Leah — but if he should carry out his threat——"

"Which way do you think the vote will go?" Stefan asked.

"Mandell and Tarov might sway it our way," Palfrey said. "I wouldn't like to make a guess. Best thing I can do is get up to date with these reports." He smiled. "You'll withdraw your resignation, I hope."

"I will not," said Stefan. "If they vote against you, I have finished. Sap, I am going out. I must go and try to think." He gave a tight-lipped smile, turned and went out of the office.

Palfrey felt quite sure that he meant exactly what he said, and knew why he wanted to be alone. Sometimes, solitude was essential to clear thinking.

Palfrey began to study the reports, and the time dragged on. He kept looking at his wrist watch, but more often at the telephone.

Would it never summon him?

*   *   *

It was an hour before the telephone bell rang, and Joyce said:

"Will you come in, Dr Palfrey, please?"

He went in, acutely conscious of being on his own. The first thing he saw was Joyce staring down at the papers on her desk; that did not seem a good omen. Merritt stared straight ahead of him, as if unwilling to meet his eye. Tarov's chin was thrust forward. The President was sitting very still.

"Dr Palfrey," he said, "the Assembly has decided that as a matter of policy and expediency, the woman Leah shall be sent out to sea, as stipulated. The Assembly also feels that in view of your personal disagreement with this decision, it would be unwise and unfair to ask you to implement it."

Smythe was smiling, tight-lipped.

*   *   *

Palfrey went up through one of the shafts to the heart of London. Dawn was just breaking on a fine, clear sky. Over a thousand miles away, under this sky, preparations were already being made to release the woman Leah. There was nothing he could do, nothing anyone could do, to prevent it. The Assembly had accepted a major defeat at the Patriarch's hands, and there were a thousand arguments to justify them.

He walked alone, even more conscious of loneliness, wishing Stefan were here.

He simply did not know what to do. If S.I.B. had no confidence in his judgement or in what he had been doing, how could he fail to follow Stefan's example?

Resign?

The very word seemed to stab.

He heard Big Ben chime the quarter; it was the same time here as in France, in fifteen minutes the woman in the coma would be on her way in that speed boat. *In fifteen minutes.*

He could imagine the satisfaction of the French officer who had taken over from him at the radiation shelter.

*   *   *

The same French officer, with an officer of the equivalent rank in the French Navy and the French Air Force, two American and two British military attachés, were standing at the jetty near Nice. This was one of the few jetties which had not been damaged in the great wave. The speed boat was already in position, and a seaman was testing the engine; now and again, it whined, stopped, whined again. A group of officers and ratings stood on a motor-torpedo boat of the French Navy, watching. The sleeping Leah was in an ambulance, drawn alongside the jetty; it would be a matter only of a few seconds to transfer her to the boat.

A French officer was saying:

"We understand exactly what is to be done. At five o'clock precisely the boat is to be set on its course and the engine started. No aircraft may be used in pursuit. All sea areas have been cleared for twenty-five miles in all directions. You have seen all the precautions, gentlemen — are you agreed that they are sufficient?"

There were nods, murmurs of agreement, a shuffling of feet.

"In ten minutes, then . . ."

The Frenchman seemed unable to stop talking. The Americans looked ill-at-ease and impatient. The Englishmen stood at ease, staring out to sea. Some distance off, the engine of a motor boat started up. The Frenchman glared towards the sound.

"It is in the harbour," he said. "It is not important."

No one else spoke.

"In five minutes. . . ."

He gave the order. The doors of the ambulance were opened and two attendants climbed inside. Soon, the girl–woman was drawn out on the stretcher; she looked exactly as Palfrey had seen her, as Higgins had seen her. The officers made a kind of guard of honour as she was lowered to the little motor boat. The roaring of the other engine sounded louder, and the French officer glanced towards it, angrily. The girl–woman was lowered. The engine was started, and ran smoothly. The wheel was locked. One of the sailors opened the throttle, then jumped ashore. The motor boat started off, as if too quickly but it kept to its set course towards the open sea. An American officer remarked:

"Who said appeasement was dead?"

"This is essential," the Frenchman said sharply.

"I wonder where the devil she's going," mused an English attache.

The speed boat was already two hundred yards out to sea. It seemed to be heading unerringly, as if oblivious of the currents and the waves. The roar of its engine sounded — and the roar of another engine, too.

"I do not understand——" began the French officer.

Suddenly, from the harbour, another speed boat appeared, travelling much faster than the one carrying the girl. Two men were in it. The dawn light showed a head of iron grey hair, sticking up in all directions, and a huge man with him. The second boat was heading for the first, as if to cut it off.

"Stop that craft!" ordered the Frenchman. "Stop it!" He bellowed at the French naval officer, who shouted orders to men in the gunboat. Already the motor-torpedo boat was moving, its wake churning white, but the real interest lay in the small speed boat and the larger one, heading towards each other, as if they would collide.

"*Stop that craft!*" the Frenchman cried again.

"Does anyone know who the guy is?" an American asked.

"One is named Andromovitch," said an Englishman. "I've met him before. The other——"

He broke off.

Everyone on the jetty seemed to draw in his breath at the same time, in a sharp hissing sound. The larger speed boat looked as if it would crash, but suddenly it was manoeuvred so that the inevitable collision was broadside on. The two boats rocked wildly. The huge man leaned over the side of the smaller one, as they were locked together. It looked as if he held them close by sheer physical strength. Two of the officers had binoculars to their eyes, but most could see exactly what was happening with the naked eye.

"*He's got her!*" an American cried.

*   *   *

Stefan Andromovitch felt the wild swaying of the boat and the harsh spattering of spray on his face. The two boats were moving at wild, dangerous speed. Unless he judged the moment perfectly, both boats would sink.

There was an even greater danger to him; that he might be crushed between the sides.

He knelt in the larger boat, leaning over, touching that

strange still figure. He pulled her by one arm closer to the side.
Spray slapped him, and fell like raindrops over her face; that
seemed to enhance her beauty.

He edged near. The gunwale cut into his stomach. The
sides of the boats crunched and grated. He caught his little
finger between them and agony shot through his hand. But
the woman was closer. He had to get his arms beneath her
and lift her into the boat. He slid both hands beneath a dead
weight; it was as if she were in fact dead. Then a roll of the
boat made her shift towards him, and he had her in his arms.
Now he used every muscle in his great body, and lifted her.
The boats groaned and crunched, but the moment came when
the woman was clear of the smaller one. It sheered away and
went racing out of control.

Slowly, fearfully, Stefan lowered his captive into the
thwarts, until this part at least was done.

The pursuit vessel was hurtling through the water towards
them, but it had no chance to catch up. If a gun was fired, it
would risk the girl–woman's life. Stefan did not think they
would take the chance.

*   *   *

Palfrey, leaning against the parapet of the Embankment,
with the London County Council building opposite him,
Scotland Yard behind him, and Big Ben in sight whenever he
turned his head, stared down into the water which lapped
against the jetty. It was a quarter past five. Leah would be
gone now, of course, and his hope of finding out where "he"
lived had gone with her. He was so heavy-hearted that it
seemed like the end of hope. Now and again, he caught a
picture of the image of his wife, but she faded. Each time, she
seemed to be trying to call out, to help him.

He heard a car approaching, but did not look round. He
heard it stop. Men got out, and he heard them running across
the pavement, one of them calling:

"Dr Palfrey. *Palfrey!*"

He turned at last.

Two uniformed men were coming from the police car parked in the street.

"It *is* Dr Palfrey, isn't it?"

"Yes," Palfrey said. He had a silly thought: that distrust of him was so great that the police had been sent to detain him. He closed his eyes. The two men were big, eager, only a foot or two away from him.

"Dr Palfrey, you're wanted back at your headquarters, at once," said one of the policemen. "I understand that there is an urgent message for you, from Nice."

"*Nice*," echoed Palfrey, and suddenly wanted to race to headquarters.

"Sap," said Alec Merritt, just ten minutes later, "Stefan and Dr Higgins took the law into their own hands. They kidnapped Leah, and headed towards the North African coast. All shipping in the Mediterranean, including units of the British and French navies, is on the look-out for them."

Palfrey's heart was thumping.

"Stefan," he echoed.

"Yes. Sap — you know what this means, don't you?"

"I know," said Palfrey, in a choky voice. " 'He' won't get his Leah back. Now we'll find out whether he'll carry out his threat."

20

CHECKMATE

ALL over the world, the ships of the Royal Navy were on the alert. Every commander and every senior officer knew what had been threatened, and rumours had spread among the ratings, too. Lookouts scanned the horizon and the nearer waters, with almost desperate anxiety. Every time a wave appeared to be larger than usual, every time a swell struck a ship broadside on, every time a squall of wind came out of the sky, there were moments of dread. All crews were alerted for action stations.

In the Indian Ocean, in the South Pacific, in the North Atlantic and the North Sea, in the Mediterranean, in the Timor Sea, in the Red Sea, in the Gulf of Aden — all over the world where the ships of the Royal Navy had their bases, these were ready for an attack which, if it came, they could not hope to repulse.

Huge ironclads, the last of the battleships and the light-cruisers, massive aircraft carriers, perky destroyers — all of these steamed about their lawful occasions, ready on an instant's notice to try to cope with an emergency.

In London, at the Admiralty, the staff was also at action stations.

The First Lord and the Minister were awake, half fearful, half persuaded that the horror would not come. Perhaps the worst thing of all was that all men in authority knew that it might — and that if it did, there was nothing that even the strongest vessel could withstand.

Reports from submarines of all nations came in, of the sighting of unfamiliar objects, but none of these materialised into anything which they could see clearly, or could identify.

Naval attachés of the Z5 countries, and officials in all the headquarters of Z5, were at the ready.

By five-fifteen, there was no report of any sinking.

By five-twenty, there was still no report.

By five-twenty-five there was silence.

At five-thirty-one. . . .

*   *   *

H.M.S. *Worthy*, one of the oldest, heaviest and most beloved ships in the Navy, was cruising at sixteen knots in the North Atlantic, away from the Scillies. It was a clear, calm morning. Early haze reduced visibility to about three hundred yards. The sea was calm, with a slight swell. There was hardly any wind. The lookouts, high in the crows' nests, had been trebled. The bridge was crowded. Officers and men stood with glasses at their eyes, so that every square yard of the calm grey sea was scanned every second.

At five-thirty the report was flashed to the Admiralty that all was well.

Able Seaman James Drabbick, who was in the forrard crow's nest, could see better with the naked eye than many could with the aid of glasses — but this morning he used his glasses, under strict orders. He was a man of forty-seven, who had a plump, good-natured wife and four children, all of school age. A happy man and a good sailor, he was looking forward with mixed feelings to the passing of the next twelve months, for after that his navy days would be finished.

He took the glasses away from his eyes, to rub an irritation out of them, and as he did so, inadvertently glanced downwards. In that moment, he saw the eruption on the water by the very side of the ship — not twenty-five yards away. He let out a great cry, bellowing into the microphone fastened round his neck:

"Wave approaching starboard——"

Next moment, there came a deafening roar, and water rose up in an enormous wall. In that same awful moment, the decks of the *Worthy* were swept clear of men. It was as if a mighty wind had snatched each man away. Then the great ship, of thirty-one thousand tons displacement, was tossed into the air like a cork.

It rose clear of the water.

After that terrifying moment, it crashed down, stern first, and dived beneath the surface in a swift, clean movement.

Above it, the sea seethed and hissed and roared. For a few minutes no human bodies were seen, only some fish, but as the waters calmed, bodies bobbed up, and floated. One or two men made futile efforts to swim, but only one was able to strike out with any vigour.

That was Able Seaman Drabbick.

He was dazed, like the others, and swam mechanically, but instinct made him turn away from the whirlpool created by the sunken vessel. He felt the pull of the undertow, but it was not strong enough to drag him back. As he swam, full consciousness gradually returned. After ten minutes, he trod water, and looked back from the direction of the ship.

The sea was settling down, now; he could see nothing except a few waves, none of them remarkable.

He turned his back on them, and kept on swimming.

*   *   *

An aircraft of Coast Patrol, in regular radio contact with the *Worthy* and the Admiralty, saw the horror and flashed a message at the same moment, the flash which told of the disaster. The aircraft flew at four hundred miles an hour over the spot where the old battleship had been, but all there were to see was wreckage of small boats, a few oddments from the ship, a few dozen bodies.

*   *   *

"That's the first," Merritt said, almost choking. "You were wrong, Sap. That's the first."

It was five thirty-six, and the report had just come in.

Joyce was in the room with them; otherwise, they were alone. The Assembly was still in session, each delegate listening with awful intensity to the reports broadcast in the Assembly Room.

They were echoing Merritt.

"There's the first . . . Palfrey was wrong."

Word was flashed round the world to the other ships of the Royal Navy, and on the instant every commander ordered action stations. Every coastal region within easy reach of ships of the Royal Navy was put on the alert. Every dock and naval installation was also put at action stations; the civilians had been cleared out earlier.

Palfrey felt his nerves at a pitch almost of screaming tension.

Joyce came in.

"Sap——" she began.

"What is it now?" he demanded roughly.

"There are rumours of panic at some of the seaside resorts," she reported. "People are streaming away from them. No one seems to know how the rumour spread, but——"

"My God," Merritt said, "I'd like to strangle Stefan!"

Palfrey swung out of the office, and stalked into his own. He stood staring blindly at the charts, especially at the places, marked in black, where ships of the Royal Navy were sailing. He found his gaze straying to the big seaside resorts. He heard a buzzer, and picked up a receiver.

It was Alec Merritt.

"Sap, I shouldn't have said that about Stefan."

"Forget it."

"I never shall," Merritt said, as if he were choking. "I shan't forget any of this. Listen to the radio."

Palfrey hesitated before switching on a small transistor radio, perfected to take all conditions down here. A typical B.B.C. voice gradually entered the room.

". . . the government sees no reason whatsoever for these measures, and advises all residents of seaside resorts and coastal areas to stay where they are until instructions are issued, if any instructions become necessary. Listeners are advised to keep their radios switched on. . . ."

He turned the radio to another station, and heard an excited man saying:

". . . *Crowds are streaming from seaside resorts in England and in the West of Europe. Roads are jammed with cars, cycles and pedestrians. The rumour that freak waves like that which devastated so much of the French Riviera would strike these coasts was spread during the night by unidentified radio stations. Government statements assuring the populace that there is no need for alarm have for the most part, passed unheeded.*"

There was a pause; then the man almost shouted:

"*Here is a news flash from Radio Luxy. A ship of the British Royal Navy the* Worthy *was struck by a giant wave in the North Atlantic at five-thirty this morning, and sunk with the loss of all on board. The complement was over seven hundred and fifty officers and men, all of whom have perished. The Cornish coast has been swamped by a wave of . . .*"

The man went on and on.

Palfrey sat at his desk with his face in his hands — thinking, yet hardly daring to think. He was desperate for word of Stefan, and frightened of what might follow next. Then suddenly, he thought:

"It's only *one*."

Next he thought bitterly: "*Only*."

But the realisation had put some hope into him.

It was now nearly ten to six, and just the *Worthy* had gone; had there been any other losses he would have known now. He stared at the chart, his heart beginning to lift hopefully. Then Joyce came in. She stood looking at him, and when he glanced up he thought for a wild moment that she was Drusilla. It was ludicrous, but the illusion was very strong. He stared at her, not comprehending. She was not tall, as Drusilla had been, she was fair where Drusilla had been dark, but there was something in her expression which reminded Palfrey vividly of the past.

Was it — compassion?

"Sap," she said, quietly, "the Assembly is back in the conference room. They would like to see you."

"*Like*," echoed Palfrey. "It's a wonder they didn't send an armed guard! Do you know how Stefan went?"

"He used one of our small aircraft."

So Merritt had not got round to stopping Andromovitch or him, Palfrey, from using Z5 facilities, but sooner or later one of the more spiteful or malicious members of the Assembly would get round to that, and begin to castigate Alec. Palfrey stood up — and he smiled.

"Thank you, Joyce."

"Sap — take it easy in there."

"Tell me this," Palfrey said. "Do you think I was right or wrong?"

"I don't think it matters," answered Joyce. "Stefan did it, not you."

"Do you think Stefan was right or wrong?"

"How could he have been right?" Joyce asked, tensely. "Sap, I'm sorry, but——"

"It's all right, it's all right," Palfrey said. He patted her arm as he passed — and deep down he asked himself what Drusilla would have said. Would she have continued to believe in him? He stepped into the Assembly Room, where a buzz of talk stopped the moment he appeared.

He thought: There's still only the *Worthy*. A kind of hope glowed in him.

He looked at Tarov and Mandell, and thought that they were now on the side of the others. The expression on Smythe's face was one almost of hatred; on Khavi's, of gloating; on Meshnon's, of resignation.

"Dr Palfrey," the President said, "are we to understand that you connived at Andromovitch's escapade, arranging for him to fly to Nice and defy the decision of the Assembly?"

Palfrey was so startled that he could not find words.

"Dr Palfrey, please answer!"

Palfrey swallowed hard. "No," he said. He swallowed again. "No, you're not to understand anything of the kind. Stefan did that entirely of his own accord. Thank God someone had the courage."

"*Courage!*" cried Khavi. "You support such action? You actually condone——"

"Mr President," Palfrey said, fighting desperately for self-control, "I believed what I said to you before, and I believe now that the only hope we have now of defeating this man is to defy him. I think he will yield to this kind of resistance. I don't believe he has had to face opposition before."

"Oh, these theories!" rasped Swartz.

Tarov leaned across and whispered to Mandell.

"— so far only the *Worthy* has gone," Palfrey went on. He realised the awful significance of what he was saying; that if news of the destruction of another ship came through then every word would be wasted, every vestige of hope would be torn away. "He threatened to destroy the whole Navy, remember. Either it was an empty boast, or he hasn't enough craft, *or* he wants to talk again."

"How any man can talk about losing a capital ship of the British Navy so callously——" began Smythe.

The door was flung open, and Joyce came in. Any kind of interruption was rare, and this one was so violent that everyone turned to stare.

Palfrey had never seen her looking lovelier, nor so excited. Her eyes were glowing, her hands were raised in front of her, as if she were in the throes of a great ecstasy.

She ignored the Assembly and rushed to Palfrey.

"Sap!" she cried. "*He* wants to talk to you. *He's* waiting for you now."

21

TRUCE

SOMEONE in the Assembly said in a soft but penetrating whisper: "*So he was right.*"

Smythe half rose from his seat, then sat down again.

The President said in a choky voice, black beard bobbing: "Do you mean the man who——" and broke off.

Palfrey fought back his own excitement, rested a hand on Joyce's arm, and said:

"There was never much doubt that he would want to talk, was there? Can you switch on the loud speakers? Then we can all hear what he wants."

"Of course." Joyce turned and ran towards one of the wall panels.

"Mr President," Palfrey said, still fighting to keep his voice steady and his manner calm, "have I your permission to commit Z5 to any course of action which seems dictated by the circumstances?"

"Mr President——" Smythe began.

"Yes, Dr Palfrey, you have," the President said. "Gentlemen — let us listen." He waved Smythe and Khavi to silence, and watched as Palfrey moved towards the desk where he had sat that morning, lifted the telephone, and said simply:

"Palfrey."

"One moment, Dr Palfrey." That was a girl, her own voice shrill with excitement. "One moment, please."

One of the delegates smothered a cough; it sounded like an explosion in the hush. Two or three squeaking noises came out of the loud speakers, before the operator said: "You're through, sir."

Palfrey spoke as if he were talking to someone he had known all his life:

"Hallo, there!"

A man said stiffly: "Dr Palfrey."

"Yes."

"You disobeyed me."

"Yes, of course," said Palfrey. He stood upright, lean, tall, imposing — but to spoil the illusion he stood with his left hand at his hair, playing with a lock. "But I learned how tough you can be." He smiled vaguely, as if trying to visualise the other speaker. His voice was pitched very low, and many who had worked with him in Z5 would have realised that this meant that his mind was working very fast; it was as if invisible antennae were stabbing out, picking up impressions and moods. They would have realised, too, that he believed it essential to slacken the tension; to make it sound as if he were not unduly troubled. Emotion could so increase tension and easily lead to conflict and anger, when calmness could bring understanding and reconciliation. "Now I've seen what you can do, and you've seen what I can do — where do we go from there?"

Two among the delegates leaned forward, staring; Smythe, pale-faced, ill-looking, closed his eyes.

"I have the quality of mercy," the other man declared stiffly. "I do not wish to slaughter innocent people for the sake of it. You know now what a disaster could come about if I wished to create it."

"I do indeed."

"I have told you that I must have Leah back."

"Oh, yes," Palfrey said. "I know you must. I wonder if——" he paused, patted the hair back into the kiss-curl shape he had never seen, and smiled; but everyone watching could see from his expression how much more tense he had become. "I wonder if we could meet and talk this over."

"*Meet?*"

Palfrey said: "May I come and see you?"

A man in the room gasped. Palfrey did not hear the sound, but Tarov and Mandell watched him, as if in both understanding and admiration. Smythe leaned back, his eyes wide open, his hands clasped together on his desk in an attitude of prayer.

"Do you know what you are saying?" demanded the other man. "Have you any conception of what——"

"Oh, yes," Palfrey said. "A very clear conception. I think you have created a world under the sea. I think that in doing so you have created what you regard as perfect human beings. In some ways no doubt they are, but I would like much more convincing. I think that you have also extended life, by your method of self-induced coma, or deep sleep in which none of the usual wear and tear on the body comes into effect. For as long as a person sleeps, so his or her life will be extended. And I think you are either Garri-Garri, who disappeared ten years ago, or a disciple of his."

He stopped.

The hush in the big room had never been greater. Joyce put her hands forward, very slowly, as if to hide Palfrey from her sight: and her lips moved in a silent phrase: "*I thought he was wrong.*"

The speaker spoke in a high-pitched voice, the first suggestion that emotion was affecting him.

"Where did you learn all this?"

"From deductions, simple reasoning process, and the indications of the past three years," said Palfrey. "There has been a lot of evidence, you know. First, the disappearance of the shipload of doctors who had been on a conference to discuss this possibility of longevity — and all the conditions which would pertain to it. Then, the disappearance of a shipload of athletes — the nearest we have up here to perfect human specimens — I mean physical specimens, of course. Then came the disappearance of a shipload of exceptionally beautiful young women and attractive men. More of such people disappeared from all over the world, and this suggested that somewhere or other there was some kind of an experiment in progress. The rest of course is sheer guesswork."

"*Guesswork!*"

Smythe leaned back, the heels of his thumbs pressed against his forehead.

"That's right," said Palfrey, easily. "Obviously you haven't been working from any known place on earth. The possibility that you were working from space stations or from another planet had to be considered, but there have been no indications of this, and we have the space situation pretty well under review now. I don't believe that large objects can move about in space without our observers knowing. Moreover, many of the top scientists who disappeared were men with special knowledge of water and under-water activities, water pressure, engineers and research scientists who could turn their attention to almost anything but in fact had specialised in sub-marine matters and water. Even the nuclear explosive research physicists who disappeared at sea or from coastal waters were men who have specialised in under-water explosions, such as the *Polaris* missiles. You see — there is a great deal one can piece together if one has some basic facts. The key fact was that you did not operate from the earth or above the earth. Practically all the evidence showed that you often operated at sea. In view of all these facts, and the inescapable one that we have found no trace of you on earth, the obvious place for you to be is under the sea. You know, sir — it *can't* go on for ever."

When Palfrey stopped, there was only that hushed tension — followed, after a while, by a rustling of movements among the spellbound men.

Someone whispered: "*Has he gone?*"

Palfrey raised his hand, palm outwards, for silence.

The man to whom Palfrey was speaking said in a low-pitched, resentful-sounding voice:

"What do you mean, it can't go on?"

"This kind of arm's length negotiation," Palfrey explained. "We must at least know what you want. When we know that, it might be possible to work out some agreement. By far the best thing is for us to talk. May I come and see you?"

There was another period of silence. Someone coughed; the President turned and glared at him.

Garri-Garri said: "On one condition, Dr Palfrey."

"Naturally."

"I will send for you if you bring Leah with you."

Palfrey said: "Yes."

"You accept?"

"Of course," Palfrey said. "All I want to do is talk to you." He was winding hair round the forefinger of his left hand again. "Is that the only condition?"

After a pause, Garri-Garri said: "Yes. Except——"

"Ah."

"You bring no offensive weapon."

"No," said Palfrey. "No weapon."

Garri-Garri asked: "Palfrey, are you prepared to surrender yourself to me without condition?"

"I hoped it was obvious," Palfrey said. "We up here haven't a chance of coming through this without grave losses unless we can talk to you. Chance has made me the best liaison officer. I know a great man when I deal with one. You could have destroyed the whole of the British Navy, but satisfied yourself with one ship. So — I knew that I was dealing with a man of great humanity." He closed his eyes, as if to shut out some evil vision: "Very great humanity," he added. "And the first man ever to rule the deep, too. *I* cannot impose conditions; I have to accept yours. I have to place my trust in you."

He stopped, and his eyes were screwed up, as if in pain.

Garri-Garri said: "You will do exactly what I told you, this morning, except that you will be in the speed boat with Leah.

You will start from Nice at five o'clock in the morning, steering
on the same course. You will have no weapons with you.
Don't fail me this time, Dr Palfrey."

There was a click of sound.

*   *   *

Palfrey took his hand from his forehead, without patting
down those ruffled hairs. "*And I thought he was wrong,*" Joyce
said in a whisper which carried to every corner of the room.
A man said: "*It is unbelievable.*" Smythe stood up and walked
slowly towards Palfrey, every movement stiff, his hands
clenched as if he intended to attack Palfrey physically. Palfrey
did not move. Mandell called:

"Smythe!"

"Do not interfere," advised Tarov.

The President's beard was bobbing, although he uttered no
word.

Smythe simply held out his hand.

*   *   *

Palfrey murmured politely to the many who came up to
congratulate him, found Tarov's handshake very powerful,
Mandell's quick and hard, the President's feather-weight; but
then, the President kissed him on both cheeks. When it was
all over, Palfrey had a light meal in his office, talked for ten
minutes to Joyce and Merritt, and then went along to the
bacteriological department of Z5. At this hour, no one was on
duty. Here in this laboratory blood tests were made on people
from all parts of the world, mostly people suffering from suspected poisons. Here, poison gases were tested; here, all the
theory of bacteriological warfare was known. Great charts on
the walls showed the extent of the preparations and of the
dangers. Palfrey, who had access to every department, went
to a long, glass-doored cupboard marked: *Incubating bacteria.*
He hesitated, opened the door, then took out two small phials.
They were of plastic, and unbreakable. He put them into his
pocket, and went out, locking the door.

Joyce, who saw him leaving, said to Merritt: "He's taken something to kill himself with, if it gets too much for him."

Merritt said: "He's the last man in the world who would commit suicide, but——"

He did not finish.

There were tears in Joyce's eyes.

*   *   *

An hour later, Palfrey was in the air, heading towards Nice. Messages had gone out, to all Z5 agents; he felt confident that word would reach Stefan, and there would be no difficulty now. He carried with him a memory of the tension in that big room, the effect of all he had said on the Patriarch, the fact that the gradual build-up in his mind had been so completely justified.

When he reached Nice, Stefan was waiting at the airport.

*   *   *

They stood at the side of the bed in the hotel where Palfrey had first taken Leah, looking down on her. She was exactly as she had been when he had last seen her. Stefan, one hand at the foot panel, rubbed his chin and said almost unbelievingly:

"She has never stirred. Even while I was lifting her from the small boat to the larger one, she did not move. It is almost as if she were dead. Sap——"

"Yes?"

"Why do you think she is so important to Garri-Garri?"

"It's the one thing I don't yet know," Palfrey said. "We'll find out." He felt relaxed and tired — as he might after a long, sleepless night. "Certainly he wants her back."

"The obvious question is — if he is so anxious about her, why did he let her come away?"

Palfrey nodded as they moved out of the bedroom into the sitting room. The window was open, and the afternoon air was blowing gently in, stirring the tassels of the sunblind outside. The scene was peaceful again. Some bathing stations were back in service, although there were very few deck chairs, and even fewer mattresses. Some umbrellas struck a gay, defiant note. Children were playing, a few people were swimming. Palfrey knew that this was typical of the scene in a hundred places — a gradual return to normal. There was one good thing: the governments' reassurance that there had been no cause to panic had been justified; there would be less risk of a general panic, now.

"I think I can answer that one," Palfrey said.

"How?"

"It did not occur to Garri-Garri that she was in any danger," Palfrey said. "There isn't any doubt that he's sent his envoys up here over the years, and most of them have escaped, a few have killed themselves. This was the first time he came into open conflict. Obviously he had to send an emissary he felt certain would be most effective, and the risk to the emissary would not seem great. The one known weakness in this man, Stefan — an overwhelming vanity, an assumption that he cannot lose. The way he reacted on the telephone, the arrogant belief that he alone can be right, the fact that he bowed to flattery which nearly made me sick — this man's middle name is vanity. And the character of Garri-Garri fits in perfectly, from what we know of it."

"You may be right about the reason for letting her come," Stefan said. "But I think there must be a stronger reason for being so anxious to get her back. One of his men was killed — he hasn't shown any hesitation in killing ordinary people. It isn't conscience, or——" he broke off, for there was a tap at the door. "I think this is Higgins," he explained; his smile momentarily radiant. "There is a remarkable man, Sap — a really remarkable man! I think he would give both his arms to come with you to the Deep."

Palfrey said thoughtfully: "It's an idea, too."

"You can't take any more chances," Stefan protested.

The door opened, and Higgins stamped in. He was wearing a pale blue T-shirt which fitted his chunky body too tightly, and a pair of old flannels, and had a towel round his neck.

His hair looked as if it were growing in a dozen directions at once. He gave it a perfunctory rub with the towel as the door slid to behind him, and turned his periwinkle eyes on Palfrey.

"So you're back. Haven't touched her, have you?"

"No," said Palfrey. "I daren't."

"Absolute miracle," Higgins declared. "I still can't really believe that it's happening." He went to the bedroom door, opened it, and stared at Leah for a few seconds, then came back and closed the door with a silence which was almost reverent. "Miracle. What's this about you taking her back where she came from?"

"I shall, tomorrow. They're his terms."

"Getting some sense," said Higgins, gruffly. "Didn't want to lose her yesterday, that's why I helped Steffy." That anyone could use any kind of diminutive for Stefan was almost ludicrous. "But to barter for a deal — that's more like it. You've got to come to terms with this chap, Palfrey. Don't be in any doubt about it. This is the kind of secret that mankind's got to have. No sacrifice too great." He blew his nose on a grubby handkerchief. "Any chance of me coming with you?"

"Stefan just suggested it."

"Well?"

"The Patriarch might decide that we both have to be sacrificed," Palfrey pointed out. "On the other hand, he specified only that I shouldn't take any weapon — I wouldn't regard you as a weapon; would he?"

"Be a damned fool if he did," Higgins said. "I would give the rest of my life for the chance of seeing this man, seeing where Leah came from. There must be more than one — *many* more than one. Will you take me?"

After a pause, Palfrey said: "Yes."

"Sap——" Stefan began.

"None of your business, Steffy," Higgins said bluffly. "You owe me this for my help yesterday, anyhow. If it hadn't been for me you wouldn't have had this chance." His eyes were glowing, his voice was almost hoarse. "My God, I can't wait — I just can't wait." After a pause, he added in a different tone:

"Well, what about lunch? I'm famished. Going to eat here or down in the restaurant?"

"Up here, I think," Palfrey said. He went across to the telephone and called for a waiter. Then he replaced the receiver and went on: "You know that you probably won't get back alive, don't you?"

"Nor will you, so that makes us square," said Higgins. "What are you looking so preoccupied about?"

"We can't understand why Garri-Garri is so anxious to get Leah back."

"Queer chap in every way," said Higgins, pursing his lips. "Tell you one thing that might explain it, though. I'm pretty sure she's pregnant. Sneaked a specimen of her blood and had it tested — no doubt about it. Think that might be the answer?"

22

THE WHIRLPOOL

THE morning was calm, the sea was like glass, reflecting the stars which gradually became fainter as the dawn spread over the land.

Palfrey felt inwardly calm.

He sat on one side of the little speed boat, with Higgins on the other side. He knew that aircraft were flying just off shore, and that ships had gathered fairly near the spot; he was to be followed in the hope of finding out where he went, and what happened. He saw Stefan, standing by the side of the jetty like a great statue. No one else was near, but some distance off the men who had been here yesterday were standing and watching.

Palfrey glanced at his watch; it was two minutes to five.

He raised his hand to Stefan. Higgins twisted round to look at the Russian, and said:

"I'll be seeing you, Steffy."

"I hope so," Stefan said.

"Don't be a pessimist," Higgins reproved.

Palfrey started the motor; it turned sweetly, at a touch. He took the helm. It was one minute to five. He stared out to sea, just aware of the drone of aeroplane engines high in the sky, and the hum of a car somewhere near the harbour.

He increased the pressure on the throttle.

"Good-bye, Sap," Stefan said.

Palfrey turned his head, smiled, murmured: "See you, Stefan," and allowed the speed boat to move.

Palfrey stood staring at the calm sea. It was like heading towards eternity. He did not know whether Garri-Garri would take his word, whether there was any hope at all that he would see this world again. He knew that there was nothing else he could have done, and there was some satisfaction in knowing that it had worked out this way, and that he had at least a chance.

Higgins said: "Palfrey."

Palfrey wished he was alone.

"Yes?"

"Don't know what the next ten minutes or so will bring," Higgins said. "Just like to say this — damn glad I met you."

"Thanks."

"Bloody nonsense!" Higgins roared, almost in the next instant. "We'll get back all right. We're going to find the secret of *life*."

Palfrey smiled. . . .

The speed boat was travelling at thirty knots, and its speed was increasing; forty-five knots was the speed he had been instructed to reach and maintain. He kept the course with little or no deviation. He did not look round at the coast. The last headland disappeared from his line of vision; now there was only a small ship to his left; soon, that disappeared. They had been travelling for fifteen minutes, and were a long way from land. The noise of the boat's engine drowned the sound of the aircraft overhead.

He glanced round, at Leah. She was lying in exactly the

same position as he had seen before, so superbly beautiful. Flawless. Was Higgins right? Was she to have a child?

The spray was cutting into his face, a slight wind was rising. The little craft quivered under the speed. Nothing at all was in front of him——

As that thought passed through his mind, his whole world seemed to explode, and he was appalled. For out of the calm sea, a great wave rose to an enormous height. It was about half a mile away, towering high in the sky, and was perhaps half a mile long. It cut off the view of the sea, and darkened the sky. There was no hope of avoiding it, no chance at all. Higgins stood up, clasping his hands as if in prayer, his chin thrust forward; he looked like an Old Testament prophet. Palfrey forced himself to keep his eyes open, to watch that seething mass of water, the top curling down towards him.

Then he saw the gap in the middle. There was a path *through* the wave. In that vivid moment he thought of the dividing of the waters in the Red Sea, and amazement drove away his fear. There was that smashing, cruel wave on either side and in the middle a patch of calm: and they were heading for the calm.

The wave was hissing and screeching about them, but quite suddenly Palfrey realised that they were in the middle of it, going round and round as if in the clutch of a whirlpool. He could not steer against it. He was thrown to one side, saw Higgins lose his balance, thought that he would fall overboard, and did not think he would have a chance if once he fell. Palfrey stretched out to try to help him, but before he did so there was a vivid flash. Instantly, a small craft rose out of the water, a tiny silvery submarine. It was alongside before he could move. The top opened, rather like the inverted hatch of an aircraft, and a man stood up. Almost at once, a second silver craft arrived, followed by a third.

It was as simple as being transferred from one boat to another in a calm sea.

Palfrey was helped into one; Higgins into the second; and Leah was lifted, gently, into the third. There was room for

Palfrey to sit down in comfort, room even for him to stretch out his legs. The pilot — if pilot was the word, for the craft appeared to have no controls of any kind — sat behind Palfrey, who knew only that he was dressed in some kind of grey-green clothes, which revealed the unblemished skin of his arms and legs.

The hatch closed. Light which was so like daylight that it did not seem strange, glowed in the tiny space. Without a sound, the nose of the craft pointed downwards.

Palfrey felt as if he were in an aircraft hurtling downwards faster than the speed of sound. At first there was the translucence of daylight on the water. He saw fish flash past, a few big ones, a huge shape which was like a shark. Soon, as they carved their way downwards, the water outside became dark; it was like being plunged into night without a moment of dusk. There was no sound, just swift movement. Soon he lost all sense of direction; for all he knew they might be travelling upwards instead of straight along. He had a sense of high speed, as in an aircraft, but heard no sound of engines and felt no vibration.

He began to lose count of time.

He had no idea whether he had travelled fifty miles, or five hundred, when he sensed that the craft was slowing down.

Soon he realised that they had stopped. He looked out of tiny windows on either side. They seemed to be hovering just as they would in a helicopter. Then he saw a silvery flash, and realised that it was one of the other craft. It was entering a huge, funnel-shaped cave. *Cave?* It darted in, and was lost to sight. Almost immediately, the second craft did the same thing.

Palfrey caught his breath, and thought: "We're next."

They headed for the funnel-shaped "cave". Quite suddenly there was blackness, a stygian gloom terrifying in its opaqueness. He felt as if his lungs were bursting. He sensed that the man behind him was aware of this fear, and fought against showing how frightened he was — and then, as quickly as the blackness had descended, light came.

They were in a small expanse of water, in a kind of

land-locked harbour. They were on the surface of this water, and the other craft were already alongside a small quay. Leah was being lifted out. Higgins was helped out by the man who had been in his craft. The man behind Palfrey said:

"I will help you."

"I'm all right," Palfrey said. "Quite all right. Was that — a snorkel?"

"A development of it," answered the man, casually. "We have a method of passing out of deep water in the Deep Citadel. When I draw alongside, step out, please."

Palfrey obeyed.

The floor was not slippery, and he had not been touched by a drop of water from the moment that he had entered the small submarine. The pilots, or whatever they were called, wore short pale grey-green tunic uniforms; they were quite dry. Higgins was being led through a small doorway, rather like the hatch of a gangway on board an ordinary ship. The doctor was stepping through. Palfrey followed him. He had to bend his head, and even then scraped the top of it against the door frame. Once through, however, he was able to stand up. The man who had brought him here had disappeared, but another man came up.

"You are welcome, Dr Palfrey."

"Thank you," Palfrey said.

"The Patriarch will see you at once."

"The Patriarch," Palfrey echoed, and just stopped it from sounding like a question. "Yes, of course." He walked on. Soon, he saw a kind of restaurant on one side, stepped through another doorway, and saw what might be a recreation room, with a television screen in it; the screen was blank. A dozen or so men and women dressed much as his escort, were sitting about. No one took any notice of him.

The guide raised his hand, and a door slid open. Two men were on the far side, and he had the impression that they were guards.

Palfrey stepped through.

Ahead of him was Higgins. In front of Higgins, standing

upright, and dressed in one of the uniforms, was Julia Shawn. She looked at Palfrey but did not move towards him, and she showed no pleasure at sight of him. By her side was one of the men like those who had piloted Palfrey down from the surface of the sea.

Palfrey said quietly: "Hallo, Julia."

She gave a half smile — little more than a curve of her lips.

Then a man came through a doorway on the other side of the room, into a kind of alcove where there was a large desk. At the corners of the desk were precious stones, on the walls were more precious stones — diamonds, rubies, pearls and emeralds and others which Palfrey did not recognise. The effect was one of fabulous treasure. On the man's head was a crown of jewels — a crown which was like a trident.

Palfrey found himself breathing very hard.

He recognised Garri-Garri, who stared at him with great intentness. At that moment, only Garri-Garri was important. Julia was not, nor the young man with her, nor Higgins, nor any of those who were in attendance. Just Garri-Garri. He stood taller than Palfrey, quite beautifully proportioned. His tunic, like that of the other men in design and in colour, was trimmed with precious stones which glistened and glittered like a rainbow.

The effect was strange; it was almost as if he had a halo created by the glow from the jewels of the crown.

He said: "Why did you bring this man, Palfrey?"

"He told me that he would give up his life cheerfully if he could live long enough to see what you have done," answered Palfrey. "He is Dr Ephraim Higgins, who sees you——" Palfrey hesitated, half closed his eyes, and then went on firmly: "Who sees you as the Master of the Human Race."

Garri-Garri said: "I *am* its Master."

23

THE MAN WHO COULD LIVE FOR EVER

"I *am* its Master," Garri-Garri said.

He stood imperiously, much as an emperor of ancient Rome must have stood, proud and arrogant and absolutely sure of himself; and in that confidence, Palfrey prayed, there were the seeds of his weakness and his destruction.

"Do you hear me, Palfrey?"

"Yes," Palfrey said. "Yes, I can hear."

"I am its Master, and if it becomes necessary I shall demonstrate how completely I have the human race in my power," declared Garri-Garri. "How long have you known what you now know about me?"

"Not long." At all costs, he must seem humble.

"How long?"

"The possibility of some such leader has been forming in my mind for years, but I have only known for certain in the past few days."

"So," said Garri-Garri. "For a few days. Do you know how long I have been planning this? Do you know how long I have been preparing for the day when I would take command of the human race?"

Palfrey said: "Ten years, perhaps."

Ten?

"*Forty* years!" cried Garri-Garri. "Since I began to think and to dream and to see the folly of human beings, to see the way they wasted the gifts of nature on the sick and the halt and the lame and the misshapen, I have wanted to perfect man. I have lived for that. I have subjugated everything in me to that purpose. I yearned to create the perfect man who could live forever — and I am and I *can*, Palfrey."

His voice rang out.

Palfrey, watching, knowing that when this man had disappeared he had been in his sixties, so that now he must be in his seventies, marvelled at the fact that he looked and behaved as if he were a man in his middle forties; as if he was indeed what he claimed to be. *Master of the human race — the man who could live for ever.*

"It — it's a miracle," Higgins said, as if he were talking to himself. "You were sixty-three when you went away."

"I am a living miracle," Garri-Garri declared simply. "And let me tell you why, Palfrey, before you begin to talk, before you begin to think of discussing any issue with me. The earth was no place for perfection, and originally creation came out of the sea. When life first began it was down here, in the Deep, far beneath the surface of the waters. Life was created here and evolved from its creation. So I realised that it was back into the Deep that man must go to find his own perfection.

"Do you understand *that*, Palfrey?"

Palfrey murmured: "I understand," and he sounded humble. It was not all affectation; in a strange way he felt that there was only humility left to him before this mighty concept.

"I believe you do," said Garri-Garri, as if marvelling. "But there is a great deal more that you do not understand, which no one could unless I explained to them. I began to live under the sea in a cave in the Indian Ocean, hundreds of miles from Bombay. There are some small islands, all uninhabited. The islands were the peaks of volcanic underwater mountains, which I began to explore. I found great mineral wealth there, and was able to afford to pay clever men to work with me. First it was necessary for us to have many airlines from the surface to our world beneath the sea, but gradually we were able to reduce the intake. As more and more men came to help me, as more and more saw the marvel of what I was beginning to do, I was able to expand. I created new caves under the sea — as I created this citadel, the Citadel of the Deep. I brought great numbers of men and machines down here from ships which were lost at sea. I brought down teams of surveyors who found on the ocean bed all the minerals and raw materials needed for the making of steel, for plastics, for the manufacture of all the goods man needs. Once I had learned to keep back the water, I learned how to manufacture all that was needed for a civilised life beneath the ocean. Do you understand that? I have created great factories beneath the bed of the ocean, factories where everything we need is manufactured, laboratories where all the men who serve me work — *do you understand that, Palfrey?* It is mine and mine alone."

Palfrey moistened his lips.

"I understand perfectly," he said.

"All that was necessary in the beginning was to learn to keep the water out and to create walls which were strong enough to withstand all the pressures of the Deep. This citadel is half a mile beneath the ocean bed. Through the world of the Deep, there are smaller citadels, Stations of the Deep, controlled from here, controlled by *me*, Palfrey. They are fed with air from the Citadel, and live off the Citadel for supplies of all kinds. Are you beginning to understand why I call myself the Master of the Human Race?"

"Yes," said Palfrey. "Yes — fully."

"I now control a world down here, with atomic piles and atomic and nuclear power. I have nuclear reactors. I have nuclear bombs. I have the means to create the great waves — and the means to control them. Throughout the oceans of the world I have a hundred stations, all manned by men who can create the waves, who can destroy everything within their reach — everything on the seas and every one of the coastal areas of the world. Each one is controlled by me, from this Citadel. Without me they could not even breathe. Take away the harbours from your upper world, destroy them utterly, and how can man live there?"

"He could not live," Palfrey said huskily.

"He could not live without my consent," corrected Garri-Garri. "Men cannot live anywhere without my approval. Palfrey, you told me you wanted to talk, and I have spoken as clearly as anyone can. You may see everything there is to see here for yourself. When you have seen, you may go back and tell your governments how helpless they are. You can tell them that they will not be ruled from the earth and will not be ruled from the planets or from space. They will be ruled from the Deep.

"And you can tell them *this*, Palfrey.

"That all men who are not perfect shall perish. What use is there for men with disease, men with sickness, men with distorted shapes? Men with crippled bodies and with crippled minds? Civilisation's dreadful mistake has been to succour the weak, instead of destroying them. Strength and power are the only forces acknowledged in the World of the Deep. There is no room anywhere for weakness. That is the ultimatum you shall take back with you. All who are not free from blemish in mind and in body shall perish. And with those who are left we shall really begin to build the world which is fit enough for men who live for ever."

* * *

Palfrey thought: He believes every word of it.

Higgins put his hand to his forehead, as if he wanted to shield himself from some bright light.

No one else moved.

Garri-Garri stood with his arm flung out, as if in command — or as if demonstrating that all he had to do to establish his mastery was to make such a gesture. Palfrey, watching intently, was startled by his handsomeness, by his vigour, by his sense of mastery. But there was more to think about, in desperate haste.

He looked at Julia.

She was frowning as she watched the Patriarch, as if at something she did not really understand. Boris was standing with his head bowed before Garri-Garri, as if before a ruler to be adored.

"I will show you all there is to see," declared Garri-Garri. "Come."

He moved towards a wall and raised his hand, and the door opened. He stepped through, into a wide passage. Higgins,

Palfrey, Julia and the man with her followed; the door closed silently behind them. They were in the middle of what looked like a huge general office, with glass walls on either side, filled with workers. No one looked up, no one appeared to notice them.

"They are the administrators," Garri-Garri reported. "They are assessing the work which is being done in the factories, preparing the schedules of work for the next period, studying the surveys of the ocean beds which have not yet been fully explored. And I will show you more, Palfrey."

He went on.

They passed through the dormitory where Julia had slept, and when the door was open that whispering voice came softly and yet quite distinctly:

"*When you wake you will obey the Master. When you wake you will obey the Master.*"

"There have been many men throughout history who believed that they were able to make sure of absolute loyalty and complete obedience among their servants," said Garri-Garri. "In fact, none has succeeded. Men's spirits were too independent. Too many thought their own way best, yet in a perfect world the only law must be the law of the Master. In creating longevity, in creating man who deserves to live for ever, it was necessary to make sure that he was free from all the stresses and strains of normal living — the deceptions of false ideas, false ideologies, all thought of independence, all thought of revolt. Has that ever occurred to you, Palfrey? That if the spirit of revolt does not exist in a man, he is less subject to the stresses of life in the Upper World? The man who does not have to think has less anxiety, less sense of frustrations, than he who must. Only *one* man need think — all others must obey."

Higgins was muttering something under his breath; he looked as if he would be sick.

That whispering voice went on: "*When you wake you will obey the Master. . . .*"

They passed the rows of sleeping people, past more offices

and rooms where there were many people, all awake — but no one took any notice of them. Those who saw them showed no interest.

Palfrey said: "Have they been trained to work only on the immediate task?"

"Each has a task, each performs it, each has learned not to waste his energies on secondary interests. Sufficient recreation, sufficient culture, sufficient physical exercise, is ordained and is enjoyed. None more is necessary. Here you see the largest of our gymnasiums and our indoor stadiums. We have small gymnasiums at all the Stations of the Deep, where exercises can be carried out regularly."

Men were running, skipping, climbing the parallel bars, vaulting horses, on the climbing ropes, performing all the tricks of the athlete in training. No one took any notice of the visitors.

They passed through another door, into what looked like a vast studio. Here, men and women were painting or drawing, some from models, some from pictures; only one or two looked up, incuriously.

They passed in awed silence through another door into a great concert hall, where an orchestra of at least sixty men and women were rehearsing before a conductor who looked neither older nor younger than everyone else there. The room was sound-proof, but Garri-Garri opened the door, and the strains of Beethoven's *Fidelio* boomed resonantly.

Garri-Garri closed the door.

"Everything is organised and ordained," he said, "even the creation of mankind. The upper world's preoccupation with the emotions which control the sexual urge is not known here. Those of our people who are most suited mate from time to time, but there is no marriage as you understand it. The children are taken from their parents and placed in the care of nurses and foster mothers. No child knows its parents, and no parents know their children. So, emotional loyalties cannot interfere with the supreme loyalty."

Palfrey closed his eyes.

Higgins gripped his arm.

"Now you shall see the final wonders," Garri-Garri declared.
He raised his hand for yet another door to open. They stepped
through into a small cinema, with perhaps two hundred seats.
They sat down, near the middle of the theatre, Garri-Garri in
the centre. The lights dimmed. The picture came on. A voice
— Garri-Garri's voice — began the commentary — and Palfrey sat spellbound, as they were journeyed on the screen
through the ocean beds of the world — beds where great mine
shafts had been sunk. Here coal and oil, ores, precious stones,
all the essential metals, even uranium — everything that man
had learned to use above the earth, was here in abundance.
Everything.

"And here, among the finest laboratories in the Deep,
physicists from all over the known world give of their best to
serve the cause. . . ."

Palfrey saw the faces of men who had disappeared; the faces
of men who had vanished in the ships. The faces of Fumagi
Kyma, the American bacteriologist, of Professor Herbert
Rackley, the Australian atomic research worker who specialised in hydro-electric and atomic energy plants, Sigismund
Dahl, the Swedish genius in the treatment of heart diseases,
John Smith, whose work on electronic computors was out-
standing, Otto Schumacher, the specialist in under-water
machines, Patrick Mullahy, whose work in steel . . .

These Palfrey knew on sight, for he had studied their faces
so recently.

There were countless others, working as they would have
worked above the Deep, in the normal, natural world of man.
They seemed intent on what they were doing. They had many
assistants. They seemed to lack no machines. But there was
no expression on the faces of any of the men — they did
not smile, they seemed to be weighed down by some great
burden.

A man appeared in a small laboratory, a man with a helpless look on his face, a look of utter despair. He was standing
at a work bench. Several assistants, men and women, were

near him, but he appeared to be oblivious. He seemed almost
to be dying on his feet.

Julia exclaimed: "*Timmy!*"

It was Professor Corvell. Palfrey's heart seemed to freeze.

"Timmy," Julia repeated with a wild note in her voice. She
went towards Garri-Garri, one hand raised. "What have you
done to him? What has happened——"

"Julia!" The man Boris snatched at her arm as if he were
afraid that she would touch the Patriarch.

"*What have you done to him?*" she cried.

"He is one of the more difficult newcomers," Garri-Garri
said. "We needed him urgently, and were unable to submit
him to the normal processes of conversion for a long enough
period. He was much more resistant than most people. In a
few days, he will be amenable — at the moment he desires
only freedom. Some men with strong and independent minds
find it more difficult to accept the conditions, but they learn —
they soon learn. They learn," he added with a sardonic smile,
"in their sleep. I will show you how mercifully I can help
Corvell."

He raised his hand. A door opened. The drone of machinery,
the movement of men and women, the sound of muted voices,
all came clearly. Professor Corvell stared at Garri-Garri as he
went through, and approached him almost as if he could not
resist.

Before he reached the Master, his eyes began to droop. The
expression of despair faded. He looked quite blank, like a man
who had been drugged. It was a case of instant hypnosis far
quicker than Palfrey had ever seen.

"Boris," the Master said, "take him to the Room of Sleep.
He is not to be brought out of coma for twenty-four hours. I
am to see him myself before he is allowed to work again."

"I will take him," Boris said.

Julia cried: "No!" She flung herself between Boris and the
Professor. The horror in her eyes was like the horror that had
been in Corvell's. Palfrey felt sure that he knew why; she had
been subjected to the coma, she had spent some time in that

Room of Sleep, with that insistent order throbbing through
her head hour after hour, but she had not been a good subject;
she had a deep core of resistance, like Corvell. "Don't take
him there! You'll destroy him, you'll destroy him utterly."

Garri-Garri said coldly: "And take the woman, too."

24

SUBMIT?

"So you see," said Garri-Garri, "that I am the source of all
strength as well as all life."

They were back in the room where he had received them.
Chairs had been brought up, and Palfrey, sitting in one which
had looked quite ordinary, felt its almost sensuous comfort.
By his side was a glass of what Garri-Garri called wine; it was
like nectar.

Higgins was sitting with his head back, and his eyes closed.
Shocked?

"Yes, I see," Palfrey admitted. "I think I have seen everything."

"I hoped you would feel like that," said Garri-Garri. "Now
you may return to the Upper World, and tell them what you
know. Tell them that there is no known way of tracing this
Citadel. It is protected by devices which no one beyond the
Deep has yet discovered. Remind them that no matter where
I meet resistance I can crush it within twelve hours. That is
the maximum time it will ever take to place in position and
detonate a bomb which will create one of the destructive waves.
And tell them, Palfrey, that nothing I have yet shown to the
Upper World is one hundredth part as powerful as what I can
reveal. Do you understand that?"

"Perfectly," Palfrey said.

He felt as if he were in a kind of prison the door of which
would never unlock.

"The difference between the bombs I have used and the bombs I have at my disposal is as great as the difference between the bomb which destroyed Hiroshima and one of a hundred megatons. In my hands there is a strength the Upper World cannot overcome."

Palfrey said: "It won't be easy to convince them."

"You *must* convince them."

"Yes," said Palfrey, as if speaking with an effort. "I must——" he broke off. "Will you forgive me if I make a suggestion?"

"I am glad to hear you put it that way. Proceed."

"If Dr Higgins and I can stay here for a few days," Palfrey said, "if he can make clinical and laboratory tests, without being — converted, as you say — if he can afterwards come back with me, that would help to convince a sceptical world. And — there is Corvell."

"What about Corvell?" Garri-Garri's voice sharpened.

"If he could be brought back to normal, and allowed to inspect some of the research establishments you showed on the films, he will acquire the scientific and technical knowledge to explain what he has seen to the technicians and the physicists above. They might believe that I am suffering under emotional stress or else that I am exaggerating with a layman's ignorance. Men of the stature of Dr Higgins and Professor Corvell could convince them."

"It shall be as you say," Garri-Garri decided. "You shall have precisely one week."

*　　　*　　　*

One week. . . .

*　　　*　　　*

In that week, Palfrey crowded more experiences than ever in his life. He went with Higgins and Corvell everywhere. He saw Corvell change from a man at first subdued, frightened and unsure of himself to a scientist who marvelled. He sensed the intellectual wonder of these two men, as well as their emotional and human horror at what was being done here. He saw the Hall of Creation, where the mating couples had their brief ecstasy, none knowing who had fathered any child.

He saw how perfect bodies and perfect mechanical minds were gradually developed, at the expense only of freedom of thought and of independence of mind. He saw how this world of the Deep was a world of mindless men, robbed of emotion, de-humanised. He saw more and more how completely Garri-Garri had it under control, how the air channels to the Strongholds were operated. He saw, too, the communication system with the Strongholds — a communication system as complex and as effective as the one gradually being built up in space.

He saw the untold riches beneath the sea, wealth so great that nations on earth would grovel for one thousandth part of it. He saw how the oceans could be controlled and commanded, how they could be used to provide power while atomic reactors were saved for other work. He saw how seaweed, plankton and other vegetable growth on the sea bed could be processed to make the gossamer-like cloth worn by the citizens of the Deep.

Each day, he spent some time with Garri-Garri.

He did not see Julia again, but he saw the man, Boris, who had been with her. Boris and two others were always with him and with Higgins and Corvell; they were never left alone, and by night they slept in a room with two of the men of the Deep.

For six days, they laboured.

On the seventh day, they were summoned to the Patriarch's presence.

This time, he was not alone; Leah was with him.

She wore a gown, longer than most of those worn here. It shimmered and scintillated with precious stones, as if it were made of a kind of sequin. She wore a trident crown, like Garri-Garri's. She sat at his right hand, smiling as she had once smiled at Palfrey from a bed in a hotel in Nice.

"You see now why it was essential to have Leah back with

me," Garri-Garri said. "She is the most perfect of all the women here, and the one whom I knew would be absolutely proof against anything you could do. She alone has some share in the command of the Deep, she alone could reason with you, and talk for me, because she is my consort. No one else shares all my knowledge, no one else has the freedom of mind to act for me independently. And she carries my child, the one child whose parentage will be known to all. She will help me to create a dynasty that will last for ever." He was sitting at the desk, handsome, impressive, arrogant — hateful. "I will admit one thing, Palfrey. I did not think it would be possible for you to hold her against *my* will. You do not know how distressed I was when I discovered what had happened."

"No," Palfrey said. "No. I can believe that."

"Have you seen all you wish to see?"

"Everything."

"Dr Higgins?"

"More," Higgins said, gruffly. "A damned sight more. Now that I've seen the cost, if I had my way I would let in the ocean, and wipe out this hell. You were right, Palfrey."

"I am not interested in your prejudices, Dr Higgins," said Garri-Garri, superciliously. "Are you convinced that I have discovered this secret of longevity? Have you satisfied yourself that among the people moving about the Deep, people who appear to be in their early twenties, there are men fifty and sixty years old? Do you realise that——"

"I'm convinced," Higgins interrupted. "I wish to God I wasn't, but I'm convinced."

"Professor?" said Garri-Garri.

"Yes," said Professor Corvell, heavily. "Yes, I have seen all I need to convince everyone I know that you have made a hundred years progress ahead of us. Yes, I know. I've seen your listening stations. I'm satisfied that there is no way of locating your position. I'm also satisfied that you control all your stations from here and by submarines based here, and that there isn't a coast line, a sea, a lake or an ocean in the world which you can't operate in. Oh, I'm satisfied."

"That is all that matters," Garri-Garri said. "And are you, Palfrey?"

"Yes."

"Then go to the Upper World, and talk to your leaders. I will give you one week, just one more week, before I talk to you again. There is to be no argument. Whatever I want I must have, and the first thing I shall require is the destruction of all weapons of war. The second — the destruction of all the unfit, all the mentally sick, all the crippled people, men, women and children. It will be a slow process, and a painful one for some of you, but gradually you will be rewarded with the perfect world in which man shall never die."

* * *

Into the silence which followed, Corvell moved, his clothes rustling. He looked straight into the eyes of the Patriarch, saying:

"Will you grant me one favour?"

"What is it you desire?"

"Will you release Julia Shawn with us?"

Garri-Garri frowned, hesitated, shook his head ponderously, and said: "If you return with an undertaking that there will be no resistance to any of my campaigns, the assurance that the Upper World will not fight against me, *then* she may come with you, if she wishes."

Corvell closed his eyes.

* * *

There was a great wave, a roaring and a seething. When the waters of the North Sea quietened, Palfrey, Higgins and Corvell were on a small boat not far from the white cliffs of England. Near them was the wreckage of a trawler, caught mercilessly in the great wave, and the bodies of the crew floated like a menacing forerunner of what could come. The Upper World had one more reason to know its danger.

* * *

Higgins said: "There must be a weakness. My God, there must be a way of stopping him."

"Can you see it?" demanded Corvell.

"There must be a way," Higgins insisted, hoarsely. "I don't believe we will have to submit——"

"Submit?" echoed Corvell. "He might kill us off, but we can't *submit*."

Submit, submit, submit, submit——

The word seemed to be always on their tongues in a helicopter flight from Dover to London, and when they were whisked by car to the centre of the city, then into the headquarters of Z5 where the Assembly was to meet them. As they looked about them, and saw the people moving through the streets of London normally, as if they had forgotten the fear of a few days ago and had no idea of how the Thames could engulf them, they were silent. When they reached the crowded Assembly Room, Palfrey saw many different faces from those who had been here before; many different, and many more. Next to Smythe was the British Prime Minister; next to Mandell the President of the United States; next to Tarov, the Vice-Chairman of the Presidium. The room was crowded, silent, tense as it could only be.

Le Blum said in a quiet voice, touched with great dignity:

"We had messages from the Deep, Palfrey, to tell us what you know. We have taken a great deal of evidence in the past week, of the effect of the waves. Sitting in the well of the room you see Able Seaman Drabbick, the sole survivor of H.M.S. *Worthy* here to tell us exactly what happened. We have had witnesses from Nice. We have witnesses from resorts and from river mouths all over the world — and we want to know what we can do, Palfrey. I speak for us all."

Palfrey was sitting upright, pale, unmoving. He did not move even when Andromovitch came and sat next to him, gripped his arm for a moment, then looked about the big room.

"Mr President," said Mandell, "we would like first to hear witnesses tell us of the conditions in the — ah — Citadel of the Deep. Expert witnesses. If you please."

The Assembly listened in a stunned silence first to Higgins, then to Corvell. They heard exactly what was happening in the Citadel of the Deep, and judging from the expressions of these men, who had learned all their lives to hide their feelings, greater fear was being driven into them with nearly every sentence. Higgins and Corvell spoke in flat, unemotional tones which emphasised the vividness and the horror of what they had seen.

Higgins finished by saying:

"When I first heard of this longevity I thought it the secret of life. I was greatly excited at the prospect of learning more, as I have been excited throughout my life, at the prospect of giving life and health, through my work as a physician, to thousands of patients. I went with a tremendous buoyancy and with a determination at all costs to break down the resistance — the emotional resistance as I understood it — of Palfrey and those who worked with him.

"I came away filled with repugnance at what I had seen. In order to prolong life, all that is worth living for, all the humanities, had been taken away."

He sat down, amid a hush so great that the slightest rustle of sound could be heard in every corner. It was broken by thin-faced, perky-looking Able Seaman Drabbick.

"We've got to find the devil," he declared. "We can't stand by and *take* it." He was next to Stefan Andromovitch, clutched Stefan's arm, as he insisted in a louder voice: "You can see that, can't you? We can't just let him get away with it. We've got to find the bastard."

*　　　*　　　*

Corvell finished in much the same way as Higgins.

"I saw, in the films and with my own eyes, developments in atomic and nuclear power research, in the manufacture of consumer goods, in the natural resources of the ocean bed, conditions which are far ahead of anything we have here. It is my considered opinion that with his fleet of midget submarines this man can create havoc anywhere he wishes on the high seas and in the coastal regions of all our countries. He can control his submarines from the Citadel — and he *alone* can do it. He commands life down there, even the air which feeds the Strongholds. He trusts no one but himself, and to some degree, his consort, Leah.

"I do not believe there is any way of finding him. I do not believe that any developments in this world will give us the instruments we need to locate him, and even if we knew I do not believe that we could destroy him. The strength of the Citadel is greater than the strength of mountains."

*　　*　　*

"It's sheer defeatism, that's what it is," Able Seaman Drabbick protested.

*　　*　　*

"It may be possible to come to terms with this man," said Khavi. "I think we should hesitate to accept the opinion of the witnesses on his *character*. What he has discovered can be of great benefit to mankind——"

"We must attempt to find a meeting place," said Meshnon. Palfrey stood up, slowly. The Indian fell silent, the Egyptian looked away. Tarov leaned towards his Vice-President and spoke. The Prime Minister put his hand up to his mouth to whisper to Smythe.

"Dr Palfrey," said the President of the Assembly.

"We've got to put up a *fight*," Drabbick shrilled.

"Mr President," said Palfrey, in a tense voice, "I do not think that we shall need to fight. I do not think that we shall be in any danger from now on. I believe that the war is over before it really began."

25

THE WEAKNESS

No one spoke; not even the little sailor. Several men sat back in their chairs, as if so startled that they did not yet understand the significance of what Palfrey was saying. Tarov raised his right hand, sharply, opened his lips, but kept silent. The President of the United States leaned forward and studied Palfrey closely.

"Dr Palfrey, please explain," Le Blum said.

"There was one great weakness in the Citadel of the Deep," Palfrey told them. "It arose out of its greatest strength. The man who called himself the Patriarch sought absolute perfection physically. He drove disease out of the Citadel. He created a community in which disease was completely eradicated. There have been plenty of cases in the world of small islands — even of large continental areas — where disease has hardly been known until viruses and bacteria have been introduced, when whole tribes have been wiped out.

"The danger from the man was obviously so great that all I knew was this: someone must get down to him, in his hiding place. Someone had to find a way of taking disease down to him. Whether the messenger would ever return was unimportant — the important thing was to spread disease. I selected the bacteria of pneumonic plague in its highest development. There is no known antidote or cure in this acute form. It is virulent, the effect is almost instantaneous, the incubation period very short. The onset of the disease, as you know, is also very quick. I do not think there will be much life in the Citadel of the Deep after today, and because the Citadel controls the airflow to the Strongholds, little life in them either." He turned to Corvell. "I had to leave Julia Shawn there. You know that. I had to leave great men who had been taken from our world down into the Deep, men who could lead mankind to greater achievements and distant horizons.

They had to be sacrificed. The secret of the deep sleep, the hypnotic coma, had to be sacrificed. The fabulous treasures beneath the ocean also had to be sacrificed — for the time being," he added in a whisper. "All for the time being."

He stopped.

Then he went on in a voice filled with awful anguish:

"I had to kill — to kill them all."

*　　*　　*

When he left the Assembly Room, half an hour afterwards, Palfrey felt no better. Whenever he closed his eyes he saw the beauty of Leah, the comeliness of Julia Shawn, the familiar faces of great men — and he hated himself for what he had done.

There was just one consolation.

No one in this room, no one in this world, would condemn him — yet.

Soon, critical voices would be raised. He should have made some effort to keep contact, some greater effort to bring the secrets of the Deep up to the World, but — no one except he, Higgins and Corvell *knew* how impossible that would have been. In the history of the world there had never been a man of such arrogant, megalomaniac belief in his own mastery. The Patriarch could have wiped out whole fleets, just as he could have wiped out whole nations.

Palfrey felt that he himself had wiped out some of the future.

He went into his own office, where Joyce and Merritt were already waiting. Neither of them spoke. Joyce gripped his hands. Stefan came in, and behind him a man said perkily:

"Give the old son-of-a-gun me love, cock. Brilliant, that was — absolutely brilliant. Even old Monty wouldn't 've thought of it."

Higgins came in, followed by Corvell.

"I would never have believed it, but you were right, Palfrey," Higgins said. "Absolutely right. Why didn't you tell me what you were planning?"

"You might have felt that the cost was worth the discovery," said Palfrey. "You did, at first."

After a pause, Higgins shrugged:

"I didn't have the sense to see the cost. Well! I'm going up top. I want some fresh air. I'll see you." He shook hands, and nearly cracked Palfrey's fingers. Corvell, not saying a word, wrung his hand also. Then, with Stefan, Palfrey went up to the Upper World. He and Stefan and all the members of Z5 here lived like troglodytes; the Upper World was much the same to them as it was — as it *had been* — to Garri-Garri.

They walked the busy, noisy streets of London on a clear, cool summer's day, and soon found themselves by the Embankment at Westminster Bridge. They leaned against it and looked into the calm river. Palfrey was thinking that at high tide one of the midget submarines could have come as far as this, could have flooded the whole of central London, and God knew what other destruction it might have caused.

"Sap," Stefan said, "in the history of the world no man has taken greater responsibility than you did down there. You don't need me to tell you that you were right. You don't need me to tell you that you have strengthened the world as you have strengthened Z5."

"I hope so," Palfrey said huskily. "God knows I hope so."

When he looked into the smiling water of the river he could picture the Citadel as it must be now. He could picture the men and women, struck down so quickly, without realising what had happened. He could picture Julia. He could picture the silence, the stillness, the death of the Deep. He did not believe that another word would ever come from there.

And it did not.